Picture Perfect

Picture Perfect
Silver Lining Book Two

Katie Charles

Praise for Katie Charles

Art
REQUIRES HEART
#SupportArtistsNotAI
www.GailDelaney.com

To Doctor Ken

You put up with me as I wrote this. Through all my questions that had to do with this book, through all the times I had a breakthrough moment, and when I sat in class frustrated because of writer's block.

This book is being dedicated to you because as much as I was acting weird while writing this, you answered my questions and let me bounce ideas off of you (As much as you didn't know it at the time.) This is a thank you for dealing with me.

I'm normal, I promise. Well, as normal as anyone.

To My Uncle Ryan

You were so much more than an uncle, you were very much my older brother. And in all the phone calls we shared at odd hours of the day, you told me you saw me as a sister and not a niece/goddaughter. You were only twelve years older than me.

Your passing during the time I was writing this book broke my heart, and caused me to put this book, the book of recovery, on hold while I recovered myself.

This book is for you because it helped me recover while I was writing. I will always miss and love you. And this book is a tribute to how someone can always miss a loved one. I may not have gone through what Jamie did, but by losing you, I really started to understand what I was writing.

I love you. I miss you

.

Book Content Expectations

Topics include grief around the death of a parent or parents, discussion of pet loss, and grief at the loss of loved ones. Discussion of a child's passing. Difficult family situations. Self-harming. Medical and emotional trauma. Mental health struggles. Divorce.

The Silver Lining Series

A young adult & new adult series about staying true to yourself.

Book One: Land of Misfit Teens

Book Two: Picture Perfect

Book Three: The Hand You're Dealt

Chapter One

Boxes were everywhere.

Jamie's bedroom floor was cluttered with crates and bags and anything able to hold the contents of her room. Her life, really. It was excessive for college, she knew, but she wanted the dorm to feel like a home, not *this* home but *a* home. Because this place was never a home.

She fell back on her bed and wrapped her pillow around her head. The house was quiet, but it was soon to change once her aunt and uncle came back.

They loved the fact she was going off to college – if they thought they disguised the fact, they were idiots – and loved more the fact they didn't have to pay for it. That was a fine line, deciding which they were happier about. But Jamie decided she wasn't going to look at them negatively for the next week.

Then she'd be gone.

Tim and Jane Meang. After a few months of living with them, in her ten-year-old head she had begun calling them Aunt and Uncle Mean. They made it just too easy.

The sound of the front door opening made Jamie's insides tense.

"I'm just saying this is *not* how we were supposed to live our lives. We decided years ago we were going to go on six-month cruises when we retired. Christmas and New Year's on a boat, not helping a kid move into college," her uncle's voice carried through the open design house with no walls to buffer his words.

Uncle Tim was the worst out of the two. He said the meanest thing, but never to Jamie's face. She always overheard it. Jamie wasn't sure what would be worse, overhearing it or having it said to her. She only knew overhearing it and knew he was being honest when she wasn't in the room. Maybe it was better than having it said to her face. Face-to-face was often a lie.

"And, I'm just saying that you need to stop harping on this topic!" Aunt Jane yelled back. Aunt Jane stood up for her in the arguments sometimes. At least there was that. "Look, we took her in because what would have that made us if we didn't? She was an orphan, for goodness sake. After eight years, I would think you would have accepted it by now."

That comment was new, and that one hurt. She thought she had heard everything from "That girl," and "Emily's kid," and a few others she didn't want to rethink about, but an equivalent of "the poor orphaned girl?" That made her sound like the musical *Annie*. She hated that movie, but at least Annie had a happy ending. College seemed like her happy ending, with no more comments being heard through open doors.

"All I can say is thank God for this school getting her out of our hair. At least until next summer," Uncle Tim said.

Summer next year? Yeah, the school was in New York, but what about Thanksgiving and Christmas break? Getting off the bed, Jamie walked to the door so she could hear better what they said. Her mind was blank. They seemed to be pulling out all the cards today, digging the knife in deeper and deeper each time they spoke. This shouldn't have affected her, she should have expected it. It had been eight years since she came to live in this house, and their vaguely disguised resentment was all she could remember. Maybe it was going off to college that made this hurt. Her friends from high school said they were having more family time with the summer coming to an end, maybe she wanted that. No, why would she want that? Not from Tim and Jane.

"Tim, please. We've done fine by her, and besides, with the trust my sister set up for her, it's not like she's a burden to us financially. School is paid for, and none of it is from us. Just let it be," Aunt Jane said. "And besides, she's not technically our problem anymore now that she's eighteen."

What did that have anything to do with anything?

"Let's plan a cruise. A nice long one," Uncle Tim said.

Jamie never felt this low before. These words were new and they hurt. She'd known they didn't want a kid to deal with, but thought that was where it ended. Apparently not. They hated her and only took her in to protect their image. The way others saw them. It had nothing to do with her. Loving her. Wanting her. Not ever.

Screw Christmas time. Screw *them!* She would find someplace to go for those few weeks. If her family didn't want her, then she didn't want them. At that moment she felt very, very alone. The anger came second. Not wanting to hear what they were saying anymore, she walked to the back of the room and put her hair in a bun to go downstairs. She was going to act like she heard nothing, like she spent the past few minutes packing not figuring out her life, or what it was supposed to be. She needed to get out.

There were still some things she needed for school. She hoped Uncle Tim would just hand over the card, like he had for the past few years, and she could just go.

"Hello, Jamie. What are you doing?" Jane spoke kindly, her normal tone, but Jamie now knew it was fake.

"I thought I'd go shopping. All the freshmen dorms have a shared kitchen, and I want some pots so I'm not living off of the food from the cafe all the time."

This was true but she wanted to buy more than just pots. Her favorite home goods store had some great college accessories. She wouldn't go crazy, just enough to annoy them. They kind of deserved it. They hated her, right? Her intention wasn't to add gas to the fire, just some more wood. She wanted to know how they really felt, and this seemed like the only way she could.

"Here, take the Visa," Tim said handing her the card, just what she wanted.

"Thank you." Not looking back she walked out the door to her truck.

FIRST DAY OF LIVING ON A COLLEGE CAMPUS. SIGNS ALL OVER THE PLACE said "Welcome, Freshmen Class, to Clarkmore University!" The few upperclassmen on campus were overly happy and helped all the freshmen bring their stuff to their dorms. Jamie was very happy about that. Seeing how she drove by herself from Florida to New York, she was glad to have people around, except when they tried to talk to her, get information out of her. It was odd for a freshman to come by themselves.

"So where is your family?" a red-haired upperclassman boy asked as he put down one of her boxes.

"They had to leave," Jamie lied

"Did they know there was stuff for the parents?" the upper-classman asked.

"Uh, yep, but they got bumped up in flights back to Florida. You take the flights where you can get them," Jamie said, shrugging her shoulders.

"Well, maybe next time. There will be events over the year they can come to."

Jamie nodded. "I'm sure."

"Tell your parents they were missed today, and that maybe next time they will have better luck with flights."

Jamie was taken back. That's right, normal people have their parents come to these things, not an aunt and uncle who resented being your guardians. Saying family was one thing, parents were a reminder.

"Sure, I'll do that once I get settled in."

The red-haired upperclassman nodded. "Well, welcome to Clarkmore," he said and walked out of the room.

Jamie didn't move. She looked around at the boxes and crates littering half the room. Clarkmore only had two to a room, one of the things Jamie liked. If she was going to share a room it would be with one person, not two or three, like she heard other schools were doing. That was just crazy! Jamie clapped her hands to her sides and sighed. Looking up to the ceiling, she spoke.

"Well, you are missed, always have been. I never thought I would drive here all by myself. But Jane and Tim don't have time for me. Even said so the night before I left." Jamie shook her head. Jane and Tim Meang were the only family she had left, and they didn't have time for her, don't want to see her till next summer. No one cared about her, and if her only family didn't care about her, who would?

"Oh my God!" a voice rang out from down the hall. A blond girl ran up to the door and grabbed the doorframe on both sides. "Are you Jamie Boyer?" she asked.

Jamie eyed her up, concerned. "Yes," she said, hesitantly.

The blond girl tackled her and screamed. "It's me! Your roommate! Amy Chase! We are going to have the best time! Facials, painting our nails and having girl talk until three in the morning!" She paused, "However, we are going to have do something about your outfit. Not in season at all. And your hair. We have to fix that. It looks like a rat on top of your head."

Jamie had no idea what to say. How do you respond to that? This chick was all over the place.

"*Okay*," she said, dragging out the word. What else was there to say?

Amy jumped up and down in glee.

"Oh, we are going to have the best friendship!" She hugged her again. "Oh my gosh! We could be best friends!"

Jamie hugged her back with what mobility she had with her arms. Her outfit wasn't that bad. Jeans and a band tee shirt. Yeah, her hair was in a bun, but she always had it that way. Oh yeah, this was going to be fun.

Chapter Two

The crazy didn't end there. Amy brought everyone with her, all her siblings, all *six* of them, her parents, her grandparents. If it had been allowed, Jamie was sure the girl would have brought her dog.

Jamie felt a hand on her shoulder. She turned to look and saw Amy's mother

"Jamie, can I talk to you for a moment?" Jamie nodded. They walked out into the hall. "Jamie, where are your parents?"

And here come the questions.

"My guardians couldn't make it this weekend. They were busy. But, I can handle things on my own," she explained.

"Guardians?"

"My aunt and uncle. My parents died in a car accident when I was a kid."

"My goodness," Mrs. Chase declared, her hand pressed to her throat. Did everyone do that when they wanted to seem dutifully shocked? The woman smiled, but Jamie didn't see a genuine spark in it "If you ever need anything, please let us know."

Jamie mentally rolled her eyes. That was the one reason she didn't like talking to people about it. The pity was more annoying than anything. No one knew how to handle the news. They usually tried to imagine their life if it had happened to them, and they start thinking of that darn musical *Annie*. Well, there was no Daddy Warbucks, no happy ending. She didn't even have a dog to love.

"Thank you. I appreciate it," Jamie answered by rote, and turned to walk into the dorm room.

"Oh, Jamie, this is going to be amazing! I hope you don't mind but I took the space on the wall here."

Amy gestured to the wall that was already covered with photos. It was common space so Jamie didn't care, but how on earth did she get all those photos up so fast? It was only a sixty-second talk with her mother.

"Yeah, that's fine."

Jamie looked at the photos. Amy was in every one of them, and it looked like she had mastered the art of posing while taking a selfie. Jamie's walls were bare at the moment, but she could make that change. Just put the *Guns and Roses* blanket up on the wall and that would take up most of the space right there.

It took hours before the room was cleared of boxes, bubble wrap, and family. Jamie let herself fall on her bed. Sleep was wanted – sleep or rest – she wasn't sure what she needed, but both sounded great.

In the morning she would start her work-study at the bookstore. She figured it would be busy with classes starting in a few days, so there were going to be students who forgot some books. No, she expected to see half the school, and for the size of the school that could very well happen.

Clarkmore offered her everything she wanted, except for the ability to blend in. One thing the school promoted was its "intimate setting." Small class, two people in a dorm, small everything. That was a turn off for the school in Jamie's mind, but nowhere else could she get the location and the major she wanted. In fact, it was one of the few colleges that offered dual discipline degrees and had on staff some of the best teachers in her field.

Her degree was like a double major: Liberal Studies and Business. She could do just about anything she wanted to with that; teach, run a business, but in truth she just wanted to write. She could start her own business, not a publishing house for novels but for articles. It would be a halfway house from the author to any site looking for what they wrote. But until then, with this degree, she could be the writer. And, it would be a quick income of money. Not stable right away, but it could be once she started her own business.

Too much to think about. Classes haven't started yet. There was still time before she had to think. Jamie set an alarm on her phone so if she fell asleep she would wake up in the morning.

JAMIE'S WORLD FELL APART AROUND HER LIKE A COMPUTER FALLING AWAY pixel by pixel. She started running. The ground fell away beneath her and she needed to get out. Find safety. Running, she came to a wall. It was too high for her to jump and there were no footholds or handhold for her to grip on to. Turning around, she saw the ground falling away. She pressed herself against the wall and prepared to fall.

She did fall, too scared to yell out, and landed on her back. She was in her bedroom at her aunt and uncle's room. Twisting, she put herself on her hands and knees facing the door. There were voices. The same voices she had overheard for the last eight years.

"She is your sister's kid. I never wanted her. We did it because you wanted to," her uncle spoke.

"I didn't want to. I was thinking how it would look if we didn't take her in. We are all that's left of her family. It would look bad if we didn't take her in."

Her aunt's words stung harder than they should have. She wasn't anything more than a trophy. The bed fell out from under her. She curled into a ball to protect her head as she fell. She felt like there was no air in her lungs. Unable to call out she landed in water, but her bed hit first and pulled her down, causing her to get trapped in the splash. She struggled to keep her head above water. She gasped for air when she could. The words of her aunt and uncle were blasting, echoing. She was unsure if they were in her head or around her. The words got louder, and other things they have said stated echoing as well.

"Good thing the trust is paying us for this. We need something for taking her in."

She swam in the waves until she found an edge. She hoisted herself up and onto the grassy ground. She lay there and coughed. She needed to get her breathing regular again, she needed to have control of it. As she exhaled, something grabbed her ankle. Finally able to scream, she pulled on the grass as the thing pulled her back into the water. The grass gave way in her grip. She screamed and there was a large flash of white. She wasn't in the water, she was falling once again. She looked down at her leg. Words swirled and wrapped around her and formed a hand and wrapped themselves around her leg. She landed against stone and she gasped. It was hard for her to get air into her lungs. She felt like she was just hit with a baseball bat. Fighting to breathe, she kicked her leg to get the word hand to let go, hitting it with her other hand and scratching it with her long nails.

The hand let go of her and withered away. She didn't know what the hand was connected to. It took her a moment to try and gain her breath. Once she did, she stood up and looked around. She turned to the left and saw a wall that had writing on it. She walked closer to see what the markings said.

"We never wanted you."

She knew what it meant. It was a jab at how she was living and an echo of everything she had heard from her aunt and uncle. She fell to her knees. The ground gave out from under her and she fell. A brighter flash of white hit her.

Jamie sat up in bed in a cold sweat. She panted, out of breath. The room was dark. Grabbing her phone, she looked at the time.

Two-thirty.

She looked to see if she had woken up Amy. No, she wasn't moving or showing any signs of waking up. Letting out a small sigh of relief, Jamie got out of bed. She had no idea what she was going to do. Going for a walk was a stupid idea. Yes, the campus was safe, but it was two in the morning. No matter where you were, that wasn't a good idea. She walked into the bathroom and pulled out her face cleaning supplies.

So something productive. School just started so there was no point to do anything else. She did all her reading already, and reading anything this late would provide no benefit.

There was a washcloth under the sink. Putting it in the sink, she turned the water on hot. When the water was steaming and when the cloth was soaked she turned it off. She wrung out the cloth so it was just damp and hot. She put it on her face and breathed in the steam

Taking the cleanser, she scrubbed her face till it hurt. Her face was lathered in soap and cleansing oils. She wiped her face clean of it. Sadly, part of her face was raw. But, it was under her chin and cheeks. It wouldn't be noticed all that much and she could cover it with make-up. She sighed and walked back to her bed. She didn't want to fall back asleep. She didn't want the dream to come back.

Her hair was down. The only time she had her hair out of the bun she was when she sleeping. But right now she needed it out of her face. Throwing it in a messy bun, she curled back into her bed. She unplugged her phone and scrolled through TikTok. It was painful how much she didn't want to go to sleep, but in the end, her eyes won, and she fell asleep with her phone on her chest.

Chapter Three

"Where are you going?" her roommate asked.

"Work. I work in the bookstore. If you get locked out or something, I'll be there." Jamie responded and walked out of the small room dressed in the uniform she was required to wear: tan pants and a blue shirt with Clarkmore University embroidered in yellow over her heart. Compared to the other uniforms she could have, Jamie was glad she had this.

She had expected the job to be more interesting, though. People came in spurts; and walked into the bookstore to see if they could find their book for the next class. Half the people didn't buy anything, took photos of the back of the book to get the ISBN, and tried to find it cheaper online. That was what she did, found all her books for half price on whatever online store she could find. College Student Rule #1: save as much money as you can. No, that should have been College Rule #2, right behind never turn down free food.

Jamie was pricing notebooks when there was a tap on her shoulder. She had drifted into her own little world thinking about college rules and how she could write a book on it and become rich and famous just based off that book alone. The tap dragged her out of that daydream. She turned her head in the direction of the tap but kept her eyes down. Not bad shoes. High tops, in fact, a brand Jamie liked. *Good taste.* Sitting on the ground, she has been able to see many types of shoes today, but not many people were in Converse.

Jamie tilted her head back to see the rest of him. From the floor, he looked tall, but then again, her perspective was way off.

"Hi, sorry." She staggered to her feet. He offered his hand to help her off the floor, but she shook her head and gained her feet. "Can I help you?"

"I just need to check out."

Once she stood beside him she noted he wasn't nearly as tall as she thought, He towered over her by only by a few inches, so he had to be around five-foot-eleven, placing him around average for most guys. Jamie was a bit on the tall side for a girl, so she liked tall guys. Brown hair, brown eyes, and a little bit on the lanky side, books in his hand. Alright so he was good-looking, not her ideal, but she had no complaints at first glance. He had books in his hand, so maybe he planned on studying and not just goofing off in school.

"Right." She tried to blink herself out of the daydream as she moved past him to the register at the front of the store. Ringing him up, she smiled. "I'm Jamie, by the way."

"Scott." He leaned against the counter, hunching over and resting on his bent arms. "What year are you, Jamie?"

"Freshman. You?" She looked at the books she rang up. There were a lot of introductory books: *Intro to Psychology*, *Intro to Acting*, *Intro the Anthropology.* "I'm going to take a wild guess here and say freshman, too?"

Scott nodded and chuckled. "Was it the *Intro to Acting* or *Into to Psychology* that tipped you off?"

Jamie scoffed, shaking her head. "Neither. It was definitely anthropology. What section are you in?"

"Second: Bond, Monday and Wednesday at three. I have yet to find anyone that's in that class."

"Your total is $294.32. And now you have, Scott. I'm in that class." She smirked and held out her hand for payment. Other people walked into the store, and she smiled at them, as she was instructed to do.

He handed her a Visa. "Awesome. I'll be glad to see a familiar face tomorrow."

"I've met a few people from other classes I have – I supposed that's a benefit of working in here – but you're the first one from anthropology." Jamie swiped the card into the computer and plugged in the required code.

"Maybe we can sit with each other."

Jamie handed the card back to Scott and smiled. "Yeah, sure, we can sit with each other." A loud thwack made Jamie jump when the next customer dropped their stack of books on the counter. "Gosh, can I help you?"

She put her hand on top of the offending book in case he wanted to try that again. Jamie looked up and felt a rush of blood on her face. She was blushing, wonderful. A guy stood beside Scott, kinda long blond hair, and blue eyes, was taller than Scott, and had more muscles. He had an air of perfection about him. Physically, he was everything Jamie was usually attracted to.

"I – uhh – Can I help you?" she stuttered, asking again.

"Just to buy this." He pointed to the book Jamie still had her hand on.

"Right." She bit her lip and slid the book over to her. "General Biology? Are you a science major?"

He nodded. "Pre-Med."

Jamie nodded. She was a klutz, so knowing a doctor even a 'pre' doctor – was probably a good thing. She shook the thoughts out of her head. No, no. *Focus on school.* "Your total is $223.00. Dang, glad I'm not a science major." She looked to him for payment.

"It's the price we have to pay," he said with a smirk and a shrug. "I'm Duncan, by the way. Duncan Buchanan"

"Hey, man," Scott said.

Duncan turned his head and gave a nod. "Hey."

"Jamie," she spoke, getting her voice in. He handed her a card, and she plugged it into the computer. She put the credit card on the book and passed it back to him. "Sign this." She handed him the receipt and a pen. She glanced over at Scott who was giving her a look of... disapproval? Duncan handed it back. "Have a good day."

"You, too," he called over his shoulder as he walked out the door.

"Wow." Scott rolled his eyes.

"What?" she asked, handing him his paper to sign.

"You played that off so smooth. The only one who couldn't tell that you were attracted to him was him." Scott signed the paper and handed it back to Jamie with a laugh. "But, that's Duncan for you."

"You know him?" Jamie stuck the two slips of paper in the corner of the drawer. She looked at him with the same look of surprise.

"He's my roommate." He shrugged. "See you in class tomorrow then." He picked up his books.

"Wait, what?" It just got weird. "Are you kidding me? Please say you are kidding me."

Scott shook his head. "Nope. Not kidding. I'll see you in class."

Jamie groaned as soon as Scott was out the door. *Great...*She knew it was bad when she had to dumb it down for herself. *I just flirted with a really nice guy, and I have class with his roommate.* Yeah, even *that* sounded bad.

"Jamie," her boss, Mrs. Scott, called out from the office behind the register.

"Yes?" she responded, hoping for something simple. Count the history books or something.

"I saw that whole thing." She winked and smiled. "I wish you luck."

Mrs. Scott snickered, from what she knew about her boss was that she just graduated from here a few years ago. So she was close in age. Jamie groaned and put her head on the counter.

"That doesn't help me much, Jade," she muttered.

Jamie sat in her chair, leaned back, and propped her feet on top of the desk. She knew she had to call, but she didn't want to. With a groan, she reached into her pant pocket, still not changed from her day of working, and pulled out her cell phone. Classes start the next day, and she should be unpacking, and setting up her notebooks, binders, and overall living space. But first, she had to make a phone call. Pressing and holding number two, her speed dial for her aunt, she put the phone up to her ear.

Ring once.

Ring twice

Ring three times and there was an answer. "Aunt Jane?" Jamie spoke getting the attention of the woman on the other end.

"Hello, Jamie. How are you?"

"I'm good. I just thought I would call and let you know I'm okay and what's going on." She paused, waiting for some response. When she got none she kept talking. "Everything is moved into the dorm, I have all my books, and I started working today." She was going to leave the part out about the boys.

"That's nice. Good to know you are settling in," her aunt said, sounding distracted.

Jamie clicked her tongue. "Yeah, I'm settling in fine." She felt like she was forcing the conversation. The door to her left opened; Amy was back. "Well hey, I got to go. Bye." She knew her aunt wasn't going to say much more so she just hung up the phone and casually tossed it on the desk.

"You didn't have to get off the phone for me."

"You were the perfect reason to get off the phone. I didn't want to be on it anymore. Just didn't have a good reason to hang up." Jamie dropped her head in her hands, the bun on her head pointing up. She had effectively folded herself in half.

"So who was it? Old boyfriend? Ex-best friend?"

"My aunt. The one I grew up with." That sounded so harsh and mean. Not her guardian, not her caretaker but the woman related to her by blood, and she grew up under her control. And her uncle. Not like her uncle was any better.

"Right. Can I know that story?"

"My parents died when I was ten," she started with a non-committal shrug, used to tell the story by now. She'd gotten good at leaving it as just a story, separate enough from her that it didn't hurt anymore. At least that was what she told herself. "They were part of a car crash." That was how she always heard it worded. "A part of" because being in it would mean they were in a car. "They were just walking on the sidewalk. Going to the bank."

"So you ended up with your aunt and uncle, whom I don't think I met." Amy tapped her chin as if she was trying to remember.

"No, you didn't meet them." Jamie sat up and took her feet off that desk. "They were the only family I had left. My aunt is – was – my mom's sister. They took me in because..." She paused remembering what she overheard. "Because they had to."

She shook her head, trying to shake away the memory.

But, it was too new.

"That's harsh."

Well, that's one way to put it.

"It doesn't matter all that much now. I'm here and can finally do my own thing." She smiled at her roommate, trying to redirect the conversation. "What have you been up to today?"

"Walking the campus. Finding my classes so I don't look like the lost freshman tomorrow; although with all the people coming in today, I still managed to look like the lost one." Amy giggled. "Oh well. Rather it be today than tomorrow."

Jamie nodded. This she could handle. This calm, yet giggling version of her roommate she could take. Not the over-exuberant one that she saw yesterday moving in. That one scared her a little bit.

She had never experienced a tackle hug before. First time for everything, she supposed. Jamie stood from the desk and walked to her bed. Pulling out a binder and a thick folder from one of the few unpacked boxes she had shoved under her bed, she sat on the bed. Inside the folder, there was a plethora of photos. Laying them before her she chose a handful and started putting them in the front slip of the binder so they formed a cover.

"I didn't know you had a dog." Amy bounced over.

"Had. My aunt and uncle got rid of him a year after my parents died. Because of his breed, they said. He was the nicest Boxer you could ever meet."

"His breed? That seems like a bad reason to get rid of a dog."

Jamie nodded. "Boxers are seen as fighting dogs, sadly. So because of that, they sent him to the pound. I don't know what happened to him from there."

Jamie hated it. Rocky was her best friend in the worst time of her life. She was still angry about it when she let herself dwell. There was no reason for the dog to be sent to the pound like some unwanted burden. He was loved. By *her*. Not after everything she had been through. She was unsure when Amy walked away or out of the room for that matter. Jamie turned back to her photos and memories of happier times.

Chapter Four

Jamie sat in the second row all the way against the wall in her anthropology class. Students wandered in, the majority of them being freshmen so they all had the same wide-eyed, terrified look of bewilderment. Even she felt it from time to time. She just hid it better, or at least she hoped she did. She lifted her left foot, pushing up against the seat of the chair next to her. Her hand was in a fist and pushing against her chin. Jeans and a band tee shirt, her hair in a bun, was the normal dress for her.

Jamie let her mind wander while she waited for the class to fill up and begin. Not thinking a thing, drifting off and letting herself relax if only for a moment. So when there was a tap on her shoulder she nearly jumped out of her seat.

"I'm sorry. I didn't mean to make you jump."

She shook her head and took her foot off the chair. "Stop sneaking up on me, Scott." She smiled rolling her eyes as she spoke

"Maybe, I should sit somewhere else."

"No. Here. Sit."

The classroom buzzed with chatter. Everyone was getting to know each other. The door opened and everyone fell silent. A man in maybe his early thirties, easily over six feet tall, holding a binder walked down the aisle of chairs to the front of the room. Obviously, he was the professor, but he didn't dress the part. He wore a white dress shirt, black vest, black pants, and a multicolored scarf. His light brown, curly hair was almost out of control with how long it was, though it looked like he tried to keep it back with gel or something. Didn't matter. His face was all angles, and even from the back of the room, Jamie could see he had really blue eyes, the kind that sort of pop out and made themselves obvious.

"Good morning. I'm Doctor Bond, James Bond." He paused holding the bottom of his vest. He had a slight accent, British, probably English, but it was subtle like maybe he'd only spent a little time there or hadn't been in England in a long time. "Andrew Bond, actually; but I always like to tell that joke on the first day of classes." He smiled and let out a laugh.

A mix of laughs and chuckles spread through the room.

"I think I could like him," Jamie whispered to Scott.

Anyone who made a James Bond joke at his own expense was good in her book. The professor clapped his hands and rubbed them together.

"Alright, I'm going to go ahead and pass out the syllabus and let you know what we are going to do throughout the term. Yes?" He opened his binder and pulled out a stack of papers. Instead of handing some to the first student in each row, he started down the first row, handing the syllabus directly to each student with a smile and sometimes a "hello."

"I think I could, too. You can tell he wants to be here," Scott said, leaning sideways closer to her so he could whisper and only she would hear him.

"So that means he is going to be a good teacher?" Jamie asked, turning enough to look at Scott.

He nodded. "Ever have a miserable teacher you knew hated his job?"

"Sure."

"How much did you learn?"

Jamie nodded. "Point taken."

The professor reached them and handed them the paper. If he heard them he didn't show it other than his grin. He had that kind of smile you couldn't ignore. You had to smile back. "Good morning," he said to Jamie as she took hers.

"Good morning..."

The only sound in the classroom, as he finished his circuit, was the flip of paper as each of them looked over the requirements.

"So, let's get to know each other. I'll call your name, ask a question, and you answer. Simple as that. I will mark down that you are here and then we can move on to the *wonders* of *anthropology*." He emphasized the words with a flourish of his hand as if he were announcing an award.

"Okay, so he might be a little too much into it," Scott mumbled with a chuckle.

"What's your name?"

Jami's eyes snapped forward in a sudden panic, but she released her breath. Doctor Bond was looking at Scott, not her. Jamie pressed her back against the wall. She swore she could *feel* the look Doctor Bond pinned on Scott.

"Scott Scotch," he answered.

Doctor Bond nodded. "Scott *Scotch*. Hmmm. And, where are you from, Mr. Scotch?"

"The city." Another simple answer.

"New York City?" Scott nodded. Doctor Bond nodded as well and placed his hands behind his back. "Am I right to assume that you were whispering about me to this young lady here?" Jamie cringed. She was going to be called out next. Scott nodded slowly. The class was silent. Jamie was begging someone to cough or speak or something, but no there was just silence. "And, what is your name?"

"Jamie Boyer."

"And where are you from, Ms. Boyer?"

"Florida"

"What part?"

So many questions.

"Winter Park. It's near Orlando."

He pushed his hands into his pockets and rocked on his heels, his gaze shifting from Jamie to Scott, and back. There was a glint in his eyes and not the angry kind. "Do you mind telling me what you were talking about?"

Jamie paused and glanced at Scott, but he was no help. He stared at her, kind of wide-eyed, but his expression gave away nothing. She decided making up something would probably be worse than the truth; after all, it wasn't like they were saying anything *bad* about him.

"We were making an observation. You're enthusiastic like you want to be here. Like you're excited to teach. I said I think I'm going to enjoy the class."

"Is that true, Mr. Scotch?" Doctor Bond asked with an arched eyebrow.

Scott nodded.

Doctor Bond nodded his head and pressed his lips together. "I'd buy it."

Then, he spun around and marched back to the front of the room.

Jamie's jaw dropped. She wasn't prepared for a professor like this. He was so out there she honestly didn't know what to expect from him. Except other than a really good class. The professor dropped the topic and started reading over the syllabus. Jamie rested her back against the wall reading along with the paper. The class time moved quickly, when Doctor Bond dismissed the class Jamie and Scott rushed out of the room.

"Well, that was interesting," Scott said first, holding the door open for her as she walked through.

"I like him. He's intimidating, but I like him." Jamie gave a shrug. "Are you free? Let's check our mail." Scott nodded and they walked to the left where the abundance of mailboxes lined up for student use.

"I heard some other kids say they've been getting stuff from their families. I guess it was part of orientation, to surprise us during our first week."

Jamie looked around at the crowded hall and gave a shrug, avoiding looking right at Scott. "I wouldn't know. I came up by myself."

She caught the pause in Scott's step next to her, but he quickly resumed walking. She bit her lip, found her mailbox, and plugged in the code given to her via email. The long pause approached stifling. Scott stepped into the space beside her and leaned his shoulder against the wall of mailboxes.

"Your parents didn't come with you?"

"My parents died a few years ago," she said in her rehearsed tone. She knew she had to get used to saying it because it would come up again and again. Holidays. Family Weekends. Special Events. It was easier if she didn't look at him, or anyone else when she told the story. "I lived with my aunt and uncle in Florida. They were...busy." She pulled out what mail she had, flipped it around in her hand to stack it from smallest to largest, and shuffled through it.

Someone bumped into her and pushed her toward Scott. He caught her from falling over and held on to her elbow until she stood again. She scowled at the back of whoever it was.

"I'm sorry, Jamie. For all of it."

Something in his voice rang so sincere it made her throat itch, and she had to swallow. She shrugged. "I miss my parents. I was ten when it happened. And, I have grown used to having my aunt and uncle being busy." She shuffled through her mail, and stopped short, staring at the envelope from her aunt and uncle.

There was a tap on her shoulder, scaring her, and she jumped around. Duncan.

"What is with you two and the shoulder tapping, huh?"

"You're the girl from the bookstore, right?" he asked, ignoring her question.

Jamie nodded, at a loss for words, something very rare for her.

Duncan looked from her to Scott and back. "Open hours start tomorrow night. You should come up. I don't think Scott would mind. Right, Scott?"

Open hours. The only times when the opposite gender was allowed to be in dorm rooms: girls could be in guys' rooms and guys could be in girls'.

"I was just going to mention it," Scott kind of muttered.

Jamie looked at him, trying to read his expression to match his tone, but couldn't. She nodded again. "Sure, I'll be there. Starts at six?"

"Six. I'll see you there." Duncan gave a smile and a wink and walked away.

As soon as he was out of earshot, Scott groaned. "Can you please stop flirting with my roommate? It's getting painful to watch." He pushed away from the mailboxes and took a step away to open his own box a few columns over, a scowl on his face.

Jamie snapped her eyes to Scott. "Painful? How is it painful?"

"You *look* like you're in pain, for one. And when you talk, you stutter and rush like you can't think straight." He shrugged and shook her head, looking at her sideways before opening his mailbox. "And, you get weird. So stop. It should be natural."

"Alright," she said, moving down the wall toward him. "I'll tone it down when you're around if that'll make you happy," she responded with an exaggerated sigh.

Scott turned his head and grinned at her. "Ehh, it's a start."

Jamie rolled her eyes and shuffled through her mail again.

Chapter Five

Scott walked into his room, dropped his backpack next to the bed, and flopped heavy on the mattress. First day of classes and he was already tired. This was fantastic. The door opened again.

"Hey, Scott," Duncan said, practically mimicking Scott's actions of moments before by dropping his bag and sitting on the side of his bed.

Out of all the people Scott could talk to, Duncan wasn't one of them. He knew they'd get along well enough as roommates, but Duncan definitely came across as self-focused. Not so much self-centered, but he definitely looked at everything with an eye for how it affected *him* before anyone else.

"Hey." He folded his pillow and turned his head, facing Duncan.

"Did you get the obligatory letters from family?" Duncan asked.

"Yeah. Very supportive. You can do this. Remember to breathe. Don't stress out." He shrugged. "It was nice."

"I got two letters. Both saying pretty much the same thing as yours, but with the added 'I have more faith in you than' and add the name of the other parent." Duncan sighed and tossed his mail on his bed.

"I thought your parents were married. They seemed happy when I met them on move-in day."

"They always seem happy." He shook his head and waved off the conversation. "So, that Jamie chick. She's hot. Maybe if she let her hair down—"

"She likes it up."

"Yeah, but it looks like she's got a lot of hair twisted up in it. I bet—"

"If she likes it in a bun, let her have it in a bun. It's her hair." Scott rolled his eyes.

"I will, geez, man. I'm just saying open hours can't come soon enough so I can check her out again. In greater detail." He wagged his eyebrows.

"Nice, Duncan." Scott groaned. "Why don't you try getting to know her? There's more to her than a pretty face."

"Oh?" Duncan said, his tone almost accusatory. "And, you know more?"

Scott sat up and swung his legs toward the floor so he could face Duncan. "Yeah, I do. She's from Florida and she lives with her aunt and uncle. They're her guardians."

"What happened to her parents?"

"They died," he said, leaving it at that.

He wasn't sure it was his place to say anything, and as soon as he said it he knew he should have left it to Jamie, but he'd said it already, and it was out there. She seemed okay when she was talking about it, though maybe too okay. He wondered about the way she didn't look at him when she told him. Since she had been openly flirting with Duncan, Scott figured he would find out sooner or later. The idea grated on Scott.

"I wonder how."

Scott glared at Duncan. "Really? That's what you're going to say? I wonder how?"

"What?" Duncan shrugged.

"Is that what you'd ask *her* if she had been the one to tell you? Not that you're sorry, that you wish her the best. When did it happen? No, you're going to ask how."

"I'm not asking her, I'm asking you."

Scott shook his head and huffed. He hoped if Duncan was as interested in Jamie as she was in him – Scott winced in frustration again – he hoped Duncan got a clue.

Scott flopped back onto his bed and rolled on his side, his back to Duncan. "I'm going to take a nap before dinner."

He was done talking.

JAMIE HAD OPENED AND READ EVERY PIECE OF MAIL SHE HAD — EXCEPT the one from her aunt and uncle. A big part of her didn't even want to. She knew it would be written nice and polite, and it would all be positive things. That's what they wanted her to hear, and that was what they would be expected to write.

As her guardians

Her obligatory caretakers.

She knew she was a burden to them. She knew that they didn't want her. Why even bother with putting on such a show? The people whose opinion they cared about would never know if they wrote her a letter, or not. Why put up the façade of sending her a stupid letter when she knew full well they were going away for Christmas and leave her to find a place to go all on her own? Isn't that worse than not sending a stupid letter of encouragement? Why were they doing this? Just to mess with her?

No, she was going to hold off on it for a little while. She needed to clear her head, needed to do something else. None of her classes gave homework yet, and there was no reading. They were trying to ease her into the college life. But right now, she wanted nothing more than to dig her nose in a textbook and do something productive.

Leaving the letter on her desk, she cleared off the rest of it, grabbed her laptop, and moved over to her bed. She would look around social media and stuff for a bit and then move over to TikTok or something. She never interacted with anyone; she just watched what was going on. Reposting things and looking up cute animals in the tags. If anything it killed time. That's what she wanted. All she wanted. Something to take away the time. More time used up, less time she had to read the letter.

It was stupid to ignore it. Really it was, and she knew that. But this was one moment where she didn't care. She wished she hadn't even gotten the letter. Seeing it had shocked her. Hadn't she just finished pretty much telling Scott she didn't expect anything because they didn't even come to orientation? Why couldn't her aunt and uncle just do as they normally do? Fight about her and ignore her. She had not even read the letter, no idea what the paper said, but the last thing she wanted to read was fake happiness and pride.

It was silent for a few hours. She spent time on the computer and relaxed herself. She almost didn't know how uptight she was until she relaxed. The door opened and shut.

"Hey, Jamie. Everyone is getting letters from their families. Did you get one from your aunt and uncle?"

Jamie looks at Amy from over her computer. "I haven't read it yet."

"Maybe, you should," she said, then added with an aggravated flip of her hand, "But don't listen to me. I'm just the roommate."

Amy's mood changes were enough to make her dizzy, like riding Big Thunder Mountain or Space Mountain at DisneyWorld. But, Amy was right, and Jamie knew she was going to have to read the letter at some point.

"It's sitting on my desk. Can you pass it to me?" Amy gladly nodded, taking the envelope and passing it to her. "Thank you." Amy went back to doing her thing and Jamie tore open the envelope. The handwriting was Uncle Tim's, angled and hard, the impression from the pen on the paper deep.

Jamie
This is the first time you are going to be away from here

for a long period of time. We know you hope to make something of yourself. We would say we know you can do it, but we don't think it would matter if we did or didn't. You always do what you want, always have, and if this is something you want then we know you will do it.

We need to let you know you might have to find a place to stay over Christmas. We have planned a trip, and unfortunately we couldn't get you a ticket. Besides, it would conflict with school. We apologize. If you can't find a place, please let us know. We can arrange something for you or you can stay at the house alone.

Prove to us you can do this.

We love you.

Tim and Jane

Jamie crumpled up the paper. Sure, she had overheard them planning to go away on an extended cruise, but she expected them to at least have enough backbone to tell her in person and not this backhanded way. In a note that's supposed to encourage her of all things. No, instead they do anything *but* encourage her and deliver their parting blow by telling her she is on her own for Christmas. A *family* holiday.

It had always been so special with Mom and Dad. They spent weeks preparing, and celebrating, and Mom left the decorations up until almost the end of January. Uncle Tim's family was from South Korea, although he had been born and raised in Florida, and he'd claimed for years Christmas wasn't a holiday celebrated in his country. Jamie accepted that explanation at first until her social studies class did a section on Korea one semester, and she learned he was outright lying just so he didn't have to bother. But by then, Christmas didn't amount to anything. And from now on, it would be even less.

She was angry. Hurt. It hurt more than it should have.

She felt alone and her only family left her even more alone.

We love you. That seemed like a joke.

That's why you gave away my dog. That's why I heard you talking while I was growing up about how much you never wanted me around. She bit her lip in frustration. What gave them the right to say that? She didn't believe them, not one bit.

"When do you want to get dinner?" Amy asked.

She didn't look up from her desk, busy writing out something. Jamie bit her lip to bite back the ache in her chest.

"I was thinking of making dinner here tonight," she managed to say. "There's the kitchen down the hall. I have a pot and pasta, butter, cheese."

That's when Amy turned around a smile on her face. "That sounds wonderful!"

Jamie stood from her bed, putting her computer off to the side. "I'll get that started then." She gathered what she needed and left the room, hoping Amy might decide at the last minute to go to the dining hall instead and leave her alone. She didn't want to be around people, especially not perky, bubbly people. Tonight, she was just going to sit in her room and watch the Internet go by.

She put everything on the counter next to the sink in the dorm kitchen. "Prove to us you can do it," she muttered. "Am I not good enough? Not worth having faith in?" She filled the pot up with water, turned, and walked over to the stove.

Turning on the propane burner, the lighter ticked until the blue flame took hold and flickered around the circle burner. She watched the flame for a moment, watched it flicker and jump. She turned it on high. The tiny flicks of fire arched toward the metal grate. She just watched it. It was tantalizing, hypnotizing.

Chapter Six

Jamie walked into anthropology, her hand wrapped in gauze, the letter from her aunt and uncle in her back pocket. She almost dreaded seeing Scott, who was already sitting in his spot, an empty chair against the wall in the second row next to him saved – she assumed – for her. She didn't go to open hours the night before. She wasn't feeling well, and she wasn't ready for him to know she had burned her hand. She'd have to explain, or come up with a story, and she wasn't up for it. Doctor Bond was in the room waiting for everyone.

"Hey," she said, her hands tucked behind her back.

"Hey, back. What happened last night?" Scott moved his chair so she could get by him to sit.

"I wasn't up to hanging out."

He scowled, not a deep angry scowl but one that said he didn't quite buy it. Jamie closed her eyes for a moment, then looked at him and sighed.

"I burned my hand, and I was taking care of it." She showed her bandaged hand.

"What happened?" His forehead wrinkled in tight lines as he looked back and forth between her hand and her face. He reached for her hand and held it in his palm, careful not to touch the area where the burn cream had stained the bandage.

"I was cooking and didn't watch the fire on the stove well enough."

"Did you go to the health office?"

"No." She shook her head and withdrew her hand. "I had a first aid kit. No big deal. It's fine."

She shrugged and looked toward the front of the class and saw Doctor Bond watching them. Heat infused her cheeks and she slid her hand under the desk out of view. Doctor Bond looked back and forth between her and Scott, then finally away, and she released a pent-up breath. Doctor Bond tapped the bottom of a stack of paper against his podium and began his lecture.

She sighed. She didn't want other people to know what had happened. Her RA didn't even know about the burn, or that it had happened in the dorm kitchen. So far it was her roommate, her boss at work, and now Scott. The fewer people, the better, because she didn't need more questions. It had been a stupid mistake.

Doctor Bond was talking, but she didn't pay attention to what he said. She couldn't keep her focus, even though this was one of the few classes she had looked forward to taking. Eventually, she gave up trying and let her mind wander. A tap on her desk made her gasp and jerk back, returning her to reality.

"I would like to speak to you after class," Doctor Bond said low enough only she and maybe Scott could hear.

Jamie nodded, avoiding eye contact. Her face felt like it would burst into flames. Doctor Bond moved down the aisle to his podium again. Half the class was twisted in their seats to stare at her, then quickly looked away.

"I wonder what he wants to talk to you about," Scott whispered, leaning toward her. She glanced at him and found him staring at her. "Are you okay?"

Jamie shrugged. "You don't have to wait up for me," she told him, avoiding the answer altogether.

Despite the fact Doctor Bond had called her out on her daydreaming, Jamie couldn't seem to make herself pay attention. It was Doctor Bond's first official lecture, but her mind was so distracted she kept drifting off to someplace else. Her hand started to hurt again, the gauze more an irritation than a protection. She made sure anything Doctor Bond wrote on the board or on the overhead made it into her notebook, but she had no idea what she wrote. She was going to have to go over it later that night, but right now her mind was elsewhere.

Doctor Bond dismissed the class, and Jamie slowly packed her bag. Scott said goodbye to her, offering a supportive smile, and left. Jamie put her books in her bag and sat in her seat until everyone in the class was gone. When the door closed behind the last student, a nervous knot twisted in Jamie's stomach. Doctor Bond walked around the desk, moved a chair, and sat on top of the desk. He hunched forward, his elbows resting on his knees, and he was only bent over a little bit. A true testament to how tall he was.

"So what's up, Doctor Bond?" Jamie asked, doing her best to sound nonchalant, unconcerned. Even she knew she didn't pull it off. "Um, I'm sorry about not paying attention. I just..." She trailed off, not even knowing how to finish the excuse.

He didn't speak right away, just sat there staring at her, studying her, running his tongue over his teeth under his closed lips. Finally, he spoke, breaking the smothering silence in the classroom.

"What happened with your hand?"

Jamie shook her head. "I was cooking and burned myself," she explained quickly.

Another long pause. Then he released a long sigh and sat up straight, running his fingers across his lips. He pointed at her and made a clicking sound in his cheek. "I might believe you, but I watched you today."

"I don't know what—"

"You hid your hand from me when you saw I had noticed. Your friend asked you about it, and you shrugged it off; you didn't even want him to know. You only let him see when you thought you couldn't hide it."

Jamie bit the inside of her lip.

"I'm right."

"Okay," was the only thing she could think of to respond with.

"Did you burn yourself on purpose, Ms. Boyer?"

"No..." she said so softly she barely heard herself. "I didn't mean to. I—" She didn't even finish the argument because she didn't believe it herself. She couldn't look him in the eyes and convince him of something she didn't believe herself.

Doctor Bond stepped down off the desk and crouched in front of hers, folding his arms on the desktop so he looked her straight in the eyes. "Do you want to know how I know?" She only nodded, it was all she could do. "I had a daughter. Rachel Marie. I watched her self-harm for a long time, not even knowing what it was she was doing, not realizing she was doing it to herself, and once I did, I didn't know how to help her. I had to learn, quickly, what to look for. I know the sighs better than anyone ever should."

Jamie was dumbfounded. A huge part of her wanted to let go of her tears and just cry, cry like she hadn't cried in years. How could this professor know, after only having seen her twice across a classroom, what she had done?

"Had?" she stuttered. A cold dread hit her. Had Rachel hurt herself...to death? The thought made Jamie's skin prickle and she broke out in a cold sweat.

Doctor Bond drew in another long breath, his features softened, and he swallowed before he answered. "She had a heart condition. Her mother and I had no idea. She died suddenly two years ago."

Doctor Bond looked away from her, but she saw the change in his eyes to sadness, and it broke something in her. Jamie lost it. She sucked in a hard breath and started crying. At first, she could smother the sound by putting her face in her hands, but the cold chill wouldn't go away and she broke down. The sobs choked her, shook her, and made it hard to breathe.

Moments later, a warm hand curled over her shoulder. It was a strange sensation, familiar and unfamiliar at the same time. She remembered her mom and her dad hugging her when she was sad, just touching her so she knew they were there, but no one had tried to comfort her since the day they died. Not anyone. Just Rocky. He would curl up beside her in bed and nuzzle her cheek, lick away her tears, and even Rocky was gone.

"It was the first time," she sobbed into her hands, hiccuping as she tried to talk and breathe at the same time. "I j-just needed to do something. I was going crazy!"

"Shush, it's okay," Doctor Bond said softly, soothing.

His hand on her shoulder guided her to turn in her chair so she faced him, but she couldn't take her hands from her face. Couldn't face him. He laid his hand on her other shoulder, and she sensed him crouch in front of him. She snuffled and looked up from her hands. Doctor Bond was right in front of her, and she swore his blue eyes staring straight into her soul.

"Look at me, Jamie."

Something about him using her name made her take a shaky breath and find some calm. She sniffled and swallowed, looking him in the eyes.

"What made you want to hurt yourself like that?"

Jamie shifted forward, and Doctor Bond let go of her. She pulled out of her back pocket the folded and crumpled letter from her aunt and uncle. With a shaking hand, she handed it to him. He watched her face as he took it from her, then pulled the letter from the envelope and unfolded the crumpled, wrinkled paper. While he read, she took the time to calm herself down. She didn't like the fact he could get through to her that easy, that he could trigger her like that.

"This is from your aunt and uncle, Jamie. I'm sure your parents have something different to say," he said, raising his head to look at her again, confusion digging into this v-spot between his eyes.

"M-my parents died when I was ten," she began, realizing quickly there was no way she could deliver the story with the rehearsed calm she usually managed. "I was raised by my aunt and uncle. They're my guardians because there was no one else." Jamie's voice stuttered again, and she stopped talking.

Doctor Bond refolded the letter and put the paper down on the desk. The only noise in the room was her staggered breathing and the crumpled paper touching the table.

"Jamie, may I please give you a hug?"

Jamie nodded, a sob jerking at her chest as new tears running down her face.

Doctor Bond stood and held out his hand, taking the fingers of her bandaged hand in his to draw her to her feet. He wrapped her in his arms and hugged her, and Jamie let out a long, hard breath, falling into the embrace. Something so simple, something she had wanted for such a long time. Yes, Scott said he was sorry for her and wanted the best for her, and she believed him, and Duncan didn't know. But this, this is what she had needed for eight years. She wanted a hug. She hugged back. He held her until the tears eased a little and the jerking sobs turned into hiccups.

Doctor Bond eventually let her go and walked to his desk tucked caddy corner to the right of his podium and came back with a box of tissues. He let out a sigh. "I think I understand where your pain is coming from. Your aunt and uncle were wrong to do what they did. Tearing you down, even if veiled as an encouragement, is wrong." He held out the box to her. "Clearly you have been torn down a great deal."

Jamie took a tissue wiping her eyes dry.

"They're not even paying for me to come here. Most of it is coming from money left to me when my parents died," she said with a shrug and a shake of her head, folding and unfolding the damp tissue. "I never expected them to have faith in me, but I can't read something like that and not be affected." She shook her head, not sure how to get out what was in her head.

Doctor Bond was silent letting her talk and vent, and again something she needed. She trusted him for whatever reason, maybe because he trusted her with the fact he lost his daughter. She supposed they shared something: loss.

"They...they never wanted me." She shook her head again.

"You don't know that—"

She shook her head harder and looked at him. "Yes, I do. I grew up hearing it. They never said it *right to me*, but they were bad at whispering," she said with a humorless laugh, then mimicked her guardians, dropping her voice into either a low bass for her uncle or a strange falsetto for her aunt. "This is your sister's kid we're stuck with. She's messed up everything. What were we supposed to do? It's not like I want her either, but how would it look?" Jamie swallowed hard and swiped at her cheeks one more time. The tears had nearly stopped now, but her chest hurt from the crying. Or the empty ache. Or both. "I would sit in my bedroom and hear them down the hall, or if they were downstairs I'd stand on the landing. They never tried to hide it. I can't..." She trailed off, biting her lip making herself calm down again...well, *try* to calm down.

"That's abuse," Doctor Bond said in a low, strained voice. He sounded angry. "They may never have raised a hand, but it's still abuse."

That's right, Mr. Anthropology Professor.

"Those plans they talk about in the letter...that's a six-month cruise. They started planning it a while ago and knew before I ever left Florida they'd be gone. Since they didn't say I couldn't go back at Thanksgiving, I'm guessing they leave after that. I'm alone for Christmas because of a boat." She crossed her arms in front of her and leaned against the edge of the desk behind her. The position jarred her hand and the sting renewed. Jamie unfolded her arms enough to look at the bandage. The yellow stain of the burn ointment looked disgusting. "I needed to do something. Maybe physically feel the pain I felt emotionally."

Doctor Bond's head snapped up. "No," he said firmly. "No, you do *not* need to hurt yourself. Jamie, look at me." She looked away from her hand to him. "You said this was your first time. What did it leave you with? Eyes full of tears and a burnt hand." He took hold of her shoulders again. "Hurting yourself does *not* make everything else go away. It does not take away the pain but adds more. Not just to you, but to everyone who cares about you."

"Who—"

"Me, for starters," he said, his smile finally coming back. It was a great smile, and not in a creepy, older guy way. Just honest and it changed his whole face. "And if I had to guess, I'd say your friend Mr. Scotch would care very much if he knew what was in your heart."

Jamie looked down at the crumpled tissue in her hand. "You're right. I should have done something else. I should have studied or something. Gone for a walk. Whatever." She looked at him and shook her head. "I won't let it happen again"

Doctor Bond dropped his hands from her shoulder. "I want to make sure. Will you go see someone for me?"

Her eyes widened and she shook her head. "No. I've had my share of grief counselors and head shrinks. My aunt and uncle forced that on me at the recommendation of the family court who gave them custody. I don't want to let *more* people know about my life. I only tell what I have to. I can't trust people with all this stuff."

"You trusted me..."

Jamie shrugged. "I guess I do." She tried to smile but didn't know if she was convincing or not. "Yeah, I do. I don't know why. I just do." She set her fingers on the table scratching her nails against it.

Doctor Bond nodded. "Good. I'm glad." There was another pause. Jamie focused on the fake wood pattern of the desk, not wanting to be the one to break the silence.

"Give me your phone." Doctor Bond held out his open hand. Jamie bent down to her bag, opened the first pocket, and pulled out her iPhone, unlocked it, and handed it to him.

"Good, a phone I can work," he said with a chuckle and a wink. After a minute or so, he handed it back. "You get any desire to do anything...punch a wall, study the hell out of your textbook, write bad poetry—" She chuckled, and he smiled. "because of them, or *anything* else—" He nodded to the phone. "I want you to text me. I sent myself a text already so I have your number." Jamie gave him a short nod. "I mean it. And I mean this. You are not going to be alone because of this."

Jamie nodded again. She took another tissue and dried the last of the tears she couldn't seem to stop. They just kept escaping.

She wondered if this would be what it would have been like to have a father again. Someone who cared if she was hurt, cared if she cried. She believed Doctor Bond was genuine in his actions. She didn't want to disappoint him.

"I understand," she said.

He gave a nod. "Alright, head off. Next class, whatever, then go to dinner, and take a nap, or something. Okay?" He leaned over and picked up her bag, handing it to her, then laid his hand on her shoulder and guided her to the door. "And go tell your friend Mr. Scotch you're okay."

"I told him not to wait."

"Yes, well...we shall see." He stopped her with his hand on her shoulder so she turned to look at him. "You *do* have people who care."

She nodded. "Okay. I'm going to go take a nap, then work on this anthropology homework." She smirked. "Maybe knit."

Doctor Bond's laughter followed her out of the classroom.

SCOTT DID EXACTLY WHAT JAMIE TOLD HIM NOT TO DO. HE STAYED behind, and when it was just the two of them in the room, he pressed his ear against the door. He didn't stay long though, he had heard enough. She did it on purpose. She meant to burn herself.

He left before he heard anything else. What would give her the idea to damage herself? He never understood it, why anyone would feel the desire to do something like that to themselves? What could be so bad that pain is better?

He dragged his feet as he walked to the dining hall. He needed food. He'd overslept that morning and missed breakfast, so he knew that if he wanted to make it to his night classes he would have to eat now.

He needed to think about this. Scott had only known Jamie for a few days, but Jamie seemed to have a handle on things, nothing seemed to bother her. Even when she told him about her parents, she was calm and accepted it. He'd seen some flicker in her eyes but chalked it up to the subject matter. It had been years, and she said she was okay. Maybe that was it. Maybe, she wasn't okay, but she *was* a good actress.

He had never lost anyone, not really. A great aunt he'd met once, but she was a stranger to him. Yeah, his parents were divorced, but it wasn't an *angry* divorce, not like he'd seen his friends go through. Custody battles and name-calling. It seemed to him Duncan had a tougher family life than he did, and both Duncan's parents lived in the same house. His parents' divorce just happened. They decided things would be better if they split up *before* it got bad.

Maybe that was why he didn't understand Jamie. Nothing bad had ever happened in his life. Just normal stuff.

Scott got his food and drink and sat at a table in the furthest corner of the dining hall, completely hidden from any of the entrance doors. If anyone came in and looked around, they wouldn't see him. He wanted to eat alone. To process. He had no desire to eat. He just knew he needed to. He sat there thinking what he could do. There weren't many people he could turn to about something like this. Scott drummed his fingers on the tabletop and took out his phone.

If there was anyone, it'd be Drake Casey. They'd grown up together through elementary school, but then Scott's parents split up and he moved away, and not long after that Drake's family had gone to hell. And they'd moved here. But Drake had always been a solid friend.

He ran a hand over his hair. Scott remembered Drake had a girl-friend – Amelia? Yeah, Amelia MacDonald – and if Scott remembered right, she had lost her mother not long before Drake met her. Maybe Drake would have some idea what to do, at least better suggestions than any of his other options.

Pressing the green button on the phone, he poked at a glob of ketchup with a cold fry. The phone rang once. Twice.

"Hey, man. How ya doin'? Calling to tell me *again* to apply at Clarkmore?"

Scott chuckled. "Not specifically, but if you're considering it..."

"Always considering options. Haven't heard from you much lately."

"Yeah, been busy."

"I get it," Drake said. Scott heard a feminine voice in the background asking who was on the phone. "Scott Scotch," Drake answered. There was another mumbled bit of conversation. "Yeah, sure," Drake said to whatever the girl had asked. "How's it going, by the way? You must have just started."

"This week, yeah," Scott answered. "Look, Drake, I didn't call just to catch up."

"Okay," Drake said, his tone dragging out the word. "What's up?"

"I need advice on something," Scott explained, "and to be honest, you were the only person I could think of that might be able to help."

"Okay, I have time. What's up?" Drake asked

"There is a girl I met at school—"

"Say no more," Drake said with a chuckle. "You have to convince her you're the right one. Play the violin or something," Somewhere in the background Scott heard the same female voice. He couldn't make out the words, but whatever she said had Drake chuckling again.

"Drake, hear me out." Scott gave a small sigh. "It's more than just convincing her to go out. I really, really like her. This afternoon I overheard her talking about how she burnt her hand. On purpose," he explained. "I don't know what I can do to help her."

There was a long pause. "Wow," Drake finally said. "I don't know how to help you with this one. What made you think of me?"

"She lost her parents when she was a kid," Scott explained. "I think that has something to do with it."

"You know what...let me hand you over to Amelia. She would know more about this than I do, and she can talk from this girl's side." There was some shuffling, and then a girl's voice came over the line.

"Hello? Scott?"

"Hi, Amelia," Scott spoke, not too amused that he was being passed off.

"So who is this girl, and why am I being told I will understand her?" Her tone was light and happy. The exact opposite of what he was feeling.

"Her name is Jamie. I just found out that she has been hurting herself. I don't know how to help her."

"Why?"

"Why do I not know how to help her?" This was just getting more and more frustrating as they kept talking.

"No, why is she hurting herself."

"I don't know."

"Scott, why did Drake think I would understand?" Amelia asked her voice calm she was trying to be soothing. Scott knew that and he tried to calm himself down.

"She lost her parents when she was ten," he explained. "You lost a parent, right?"

"Yeah, I did." There was another pause. "But, she lost both?" Scott confirmed. "It's kinda different for me because I had my Da. And, I was older than her. But, I guess the feeling is the same."

He almost asked who "Da" was, but remembered before he opened his mouth that Amelia's father was Scottish, and Drake had told him that was what she called him. At least he stopped himself before he sounded like a total idiot.

"So, how do I help her?" Scott asked.

"Be there for her. Be her rock. That was what Da was to me after Mom died, and that's what Drake was for me after we moved to the city. She may not say so, but she needs that person. If she lost both parents, maybe she needs you even more. Be someone she can lean on."

"Sounds easier than it probably is," he said. "Jamie seems pretty solid, but then I heard this..."

"I don't know her, or all the details, but it seems to me she's trying to do it all on her own, and we're not supposed to do things alone." Drake's muffled voice in the background interrupted the conversation. "Drake wants to talk to you again."

There was more shuffling and then Drake's voice was back. "How did you meet her?"

"She was working in the bookstore, sitting on the floor sorting books, and I tried to help her to her feet."

"Tried?"

"I don't think she saw my hand in time."

"Ahh. Now, it's my turn to give advice. No matter what, don't leave her. Fight for her," he said.

Scott could almost imagine the playful shoulder punch he would have gotten had Drake been there with him at that moment.

"Alright, man," Scott replied. "Thanks. And, tell Amelia I said thank you."

"Will do. Any time you need help, man, I'm here. Just give me a ring."

Scott hung up the phone and placed it on the table. So, Jamie needed a rock. Someone to be there for her, catch her and be her support. Okay, he could do that.

He sat there at the table more not finding any interest in his food still. But, he had a lot to still think about.

What he realized sitting there wasn't so much that she hurt herself – which still bothered him *a lot* – it was that he hadn't realized it bothered her that much. That he hadn't done something. That she hadn't told him.

"Why am I taking this so hard?" he asked out loud, tossing the cold fry into the puddle of ketchup.

No one raised their heads and looked at him. The question wasn't meant for anyone but himself anyway. Scott slumped back in the chair and scrubbed his face with his hands.

"Because, you like her, you idiot." He pushed the plate away.

SCOTT STRETCHED OUT ON HIS BED. HE HAD JUST SPENT HOURS READING for a class and still didn't understand what the book was talking about. Ehh, it was overrated anyway. Putting his hands on his face, he let out a sigh. He was thinking too much. Way too much. Once he could settle down his mind, he would be able to think right and have some idea of what to do from there.

It has been three days since he found out about the burn on Jamie's hand. She still had the gauze on it. Was it that bad? How long did it take for burns to heal anyway? Well, it had to depend on how bad it was, right? *Ugh, right back to the first question. How bad was it?*

"You're bringing me down," Duncan spoke, breaking the silence.

"Me?"

"Well, who else is depressed in the room?"

"I'm not depressed." Scott sat up and looked at his roommate, who rolled his eyes. "I'm worried, not depressed. There's a difference."

"There is a fine line between being thorough and being crazy."

"What is *that* supposed to mean?" Something bounced off the side of his head. "What the heck..." Looking around for whatever it was, he heard a snicker from the doorway of the room.

Jamie.

"What' you just hit me with?"

"Toy ball," she answered. "Nothing big enough to cause damage."

She walked into the room, her hands behind her back. Was she trying to hide the gauze?

"At least, you hit *him* and not me," Duncan said.

Jamie smiled. "Well, I was *going* to throw something at you, too, but the only other thing I have is my business accounting book." She pulled the hefty book out from behind her back, holding it with two hands, and exposing the gauzed hand. "Could probably put a pretty decent dent in your head..."

"Yeah, don't throw that at me."

"I'm not going to. I'm going through this revolutionary thing and studying from it."

"Sit at my desk," Scott said, motioning toward his empty desk chair. "I'm sitting on my bed anyway."

Jamie nodded and dropped into his chair, opening her book. They all settled back into silence, studying. At least, it wasn't that uncomfortable kind of silence people felt the need to fill and usually ended up saying something stupid or embarrassing.

"Are your parents divorced?" Jamie asked a while later, breaking the silence.

Scott cocked an eyebrow and looked up from his book. "Yes. How did you know?"

"You have a photo with whom I'm assuming is your mother and sister" -- she pointed to one on the top shelf of his desk with the end of her pencil – "and a different one with I'm guessing your father and sister." She pointed to the other picture.

Scott sat up, nodding. "Yeah, they have been for a few years now, but it's okay. No drama."

Jamie leaned back in the chair, looking at Duncan's desk.

"Are yours married?" she asked. Duncan nodded. "They look happy."

Duncan chuckled. "They do, don't they." He gave a sigh and pushed back from his desk. "Please, excuse me. Speaking of parents, I do need to talk to my mother about something." Duncan stood from his chair and walked out of the room.

Scott watched Jamie watch him leave.

"How are you doing?" Scott asked.

Jamie turned in the chair so that she faced him. "I'm okay. Hand hurts from time to time, and it makes holding things interesting," she said, holding up the bandaged hand, "but other than that, good." She smiled.

"What happened again?"

"I was careless making pasta," she said, looking back at her book and not at him. "I should know better, I know, but I had other things on my mind." She shrugged it off.

"Like what?"

Jamie looked at him without lifting her head, then back to her book. With a huff, she sat up and ran the gauzed hand over her hair, messing up the bandage.

"Crap," she mumbled. "I can never get it to go back to how it is supposed to be."

Scott stood up from his bed and went to her. "Let me help you." He pulled her hand gently to him and undid the gauze so he could re-apply it. "Okay, so talk to me. What was bothering you that much you...did this by mistake?"

Jamie was silent, watching him un-bandage the hand with much more intensity than required. Scott removed the wrap, took a few moments to look at the healing burn, and reapplied the gauze as he waited.

"I got a letter from my aunt and uncle," she finally said, her voice low. "Remember those letters everyone was getting? They must have heard about doing them and did one on their own. It got to me." Scott finished the wrapping, and having no other reason to hold her hand, let go. "Thank you."

"A letter?" he asked.

Jamie sighed and pulled it out of her jeans pocket. The envelope was crumpled and creased. *Oh God, she carried it around with her?*

"Just read it," she said, holding it out to him, "and you might understand why I was distracted."

She bit her bottom lip as he took it. Scott watched her while he opened the envelope and unfolded the paper inside. He only looked away when he had to read. With each sentence, he felt sicker. Angrier.

"This is horrible, Jamie."

"Then they have the nerve to say that they love me at the end. I can't even begin to describe how much that annoys me." His voice raised an octave with each sentence.

"I'm sorry, Jamie," Scott said, wishing he knew what else to say. He wasn't sure what he expected, but this wasn't it.

"It's not your fault," she sighed, waving her un-bandaged hand.

Scott tossed the letter on the desk and took the hand, pulling her to him and into a hug. "It may not be, but I can still be sorry."

Jamie's hands pressed against his back and gripped his shirt. "Thank you, Scott. Really."

Chapter Seven

Jamie was reading outside at one of the tables the school had set up for the students. There was a nip in the air that made her nostrils ache and made her pull her coat collar up a little closer to her neck, but she loved it. She wanted to be outside away from the drama her roommate seemed to create to fill the void of peace and quiet, and away from people for a bit, but also liked the cold air. Being cold always sharpened her focused. She had lived in Florida her whole life and chose the north for school because she liked the bite.

That and to get as far away from Tim and Jane as she could.

A knock on the table made her look up. Duncan stood at the end of the table, his chin tucked into his scarf and his hands in his pockets. Jamie dog-eared the book page and smiled up at him.

"Hey, there. Sit down"

"What are you doing sitting out here? It's November and you're sitting outside all alone reading a book?" He bounced on the balls of his feet like it would keep him warm.

"Oh, come on. I'm from Florida, and *I* don't think it's *that* cold." She smiled and shook her head.

"Either way. Winter may be late this year and snow may not come for a while, but it's still cold, and I'm from here."

Jamie closed her book and set it on the table. "Okay, fine. I needed to get out of my room for a while. I think my roommate is kinda crazy." She shrugged her shoulder.

"You know, you can come to my room when you need to get away. Scott wouldn't mind."

"I know," she said, digging her chin deeper into her collar to hide the heat she felt bloom in them. The thing was, she wasn't sure if she blushed at the invitation or the idea Scott might or might not mind.

Duncan finally came around and sat beside her. "So what are you reading?"

"A really good book. It's paranormal, so maybe not for everyone, but I like it. It's about casters and a kid that is in over his head. It's *really* good. The pet dog even has a cape." She smiled and pushed the book toward him so he could look at it. Yes, she may have rambled a little about it, but hey, it *was* a good book.

"Is it a romance?"

"Yes."

Duncan pulled a face. "I'm not into stuff like that."

She shook his head. "It's told from the guy's point of view," she said pulling the book back to her. "I'm not saying you *have* to read it, I'm just saying I think it's interesting" She smiled at him. "What do you like to read?"

"Not one thing over another. I'm just not into fantasy and stuff."

"Fair enough," she said. "I'm not all that into horror. We all have our likes."

"Oh, no, I like those because I like trying to figure out what's going on, and who will be dead by the end of the book."

Jamie chuckled. "Well, yeah, but I don't think I could handle something like that. I would give myself bad dreams." She shook her head.

"We all have what we like," he said, repeating her own words.

Jamie looked at him, kind of confused. He was talking, but not *about* anything. Just small talk. Since when did he just small talk? So she just shrugged.

"I'm on my way to class but was walking through and saw you so I just wanted to say hi." He stood from the table.

Jamie reached for the book again. "Have fun in class."

She smiled and opened her book. Duncan took a few steps, stopped and looked back at her, then kept going. Before he was out of sight, she was back deep into the book. There were explosions and death and proclamations of love; it was starting to get interesting. Then her phone went off, scaring her in the process. Sighing, she took it off the table and read the interrupting text message.

What are you doing sitting out there in the cold?

I like the cold.

She rolled her eyes but smiled. Doctor Bond would send her a text like that just to be kind of creepy.

You are going to catch a cold. Now, get in here.

Where are you?

I'm sitting in my office to your left.

Jamie looked over and smiled as she saw him waving at her.

I have fresh coffee. Just made it.

Deal. Be right there

Jamie walked into the office and placed the book on the desk with a slight bang. "He had *just* professed his love for her and was about to kiss her."

She crossed her arms feigning anger. Doctor Bond took her book with a sidelong glance to her and read the back.

"She dies in the end," he said nonchalantly as he put the book back down.

Her jaw dropped. "No! Don't you even dare joke!" She frowned, taking back her book. "How could you even dare tell me the end!"

"My daughter read that book when it first came out. She cried over the ending." He shrugged.

"So, you don't tell it to me!" She dropped into the chair across from his desk with a huff, crossing her arms over her chest. "Now, I can't finish it."

"I'm just warning you."

"Doesn't matter now that I can't finish," she growled.

"How do you want your coffee?" Doctor Bond asked, ignoring her distress.

"Ahh, a lot of creamer and a little sugar," Jamie responded, not moving from her chair. She was still a little upset about the book thing, but she'd deal. She would just make faces at him the rest of the time she was there.

"Come now. Lose the face." He handed her a mug of coffee.

"No. You killed it, Doctor Bond. You killed it dead."

He shook his head. "What if I told you I lied?"

"I would be even madder with you!"

"I can't win, can I?"

Jamie shook her head "No, no you can't."

Doctor Bond sat at the table with a groan. "Well, I did want to ask you some questions."

Ahh, crap. That was a bad sign. Jamie took a long drink of her coffee, letting it warm the back of her mouth as she drank. Setting it on the desk, she crossed her legs and looked at him.

"Shoot."

"Have you told Mr. Scotch what happened to your hand?"

Well, that was straightforward. Jamie shook her head.

"I showed him the note, but I didn't tell him the burning was on purpose. I told him I was distracted while I was cooking," Jamie explained. "I kind of want to keep it that way. It was a one-time thing, and something I regret now, and I don't want to worry him anymore. He already seemed worried enough when I showed him the note."

Doctor Bond shook his head. "Does anyone else know?"

"No."

"Why not?"

Jamie twisted her lips before answering, thinking of the best way to explain. "Why does anyone need to know? Who am I supposed to trust with that? I mean, you're different. You're like...a father."

Doctor Bond smiled, leaning back in his chair with his fingers steepled in front of his lips. Oh, how she wanted to know what he was thinking. Was it good? Was it bad? Did she just cross some imaginary line and say too much? It was frustrating not being able to read minds.

"So I'm the only one who knows."

"That I hurt myself once? And, I'm not going to do it again? Yes." She picked up her mug and took another sip. "Trust me, Doctor Bond, nothing else is going to happen to me that you need to be worried about." She smiled.

"I do worry about you, Jamie," he spoke. "I've talked about you with my wife Beth, and she is concerned, too. We worry because we care."

"You talk about me to your wife?" Jamie asked, a smile plastered on her face. Why it meant so much to her that he would tell someone as important as his wife about her, she wasn't sure, but it did. "Wow, Doctor Bond, that means a lot. Really."

"Jamie, you are in my office every other day. I have to tell her about you," he joked.

"Hey, I would still be outside reading my book, but *you* texted me to get in here." She pointed a finger at him. "A book that *you* destroyed the ending for me."

"Are you still going to harp on that?" He rolled his eyes. "Drink your coffee."

Jamie nodded her head. "I do what I want," she said, quoting one of her favorite movies of all time.

Doctor Bond feigned shock and pointed at the door. "Out of my office," he ordered. "This is an Anti-Thor comic book room. Only Tony Stark is allowed here."

Jamie smiled. "I have a paper to write for your class anyway." She stood up and took the mug. "I'll return this later. But as for now, I'm drinking my coffee." She turned and walked away.

"You better return the mug," Doctor Bond called after her.

SCOTT SAT ON HIS BED WITH HIS BACK AGAINST THE HEADBOARD. Flipping through his English textbook, he had no desire to read, or work on his paper due in two weeks, or do much of anything. He threw the book to the foot of the bunk and laid down curling up into a ball and faced the wall. There wasn't anything to do *other* than study, not even to go find Jamie. He'd gone by her room before reluctantly returning to his own, and her roommate said she was gone. Where, Amy didn't know.

Eventually, he dozed off.

He woke up with a jerk, half sitting up before his eyes even opened, startled by the door slamming shut. He sat up and shifted back against the headboard again, scrubbing his face with his hands.

Duncan threw his coat over his desk chair and dropped heavy on the edge of his bed with a loud huff.

"What's wrong with you?"

"Do you think Jamie likes me?"

A lead ball dropped in Scott's chest. He knew the answer, but he hated the answer and would love to be able to lie. Instead, he diverted.

"Do you like *her*?" he asked.

Duncan nodded. "Yeah, sure. I mean, you've seen her, man. She's hot. She's not crazy. She seems like she's interested."

Scott knew he'd regret saying his next words, but they were the truth. "You're perfect to her," Scott admitted. Duncan grinned a stupid, lecherous, smug grin. "Not like that, man. She sees your family – mom, dad, siblings – and she figures you've got a great life. Something she wants."

Duncan snorted. "Guess I've got her fooled, huh?" Then, he scowled. "You think she thinks I've got money or something? That's what she's interested in?"

"If she were, who would you be to talk? You're just interested because you think she's hot," Scott practically ground out.

"You can't tell me you don't think she's hot."

"I'm not telling you that. I'm telling you she thinks you've got the kind of family she wants, money or no money." Scott kept to himself Jamie had confided in him her own parents had been comfortably well off, and now that she was eighteen she had plenty of funds to take care of herself. She didn't need whatever wealth Duncan Buchanan thought he might have to offer.

"I don't get it."

"She wants the traditional *perfect* family, the kind of family she used to have."

"Used to have?"

Scott groaned and mumbled a curse under his breath before he stood and went to their mini fridge for a bottle of water. "Do you pay attention to anything, Duncan? Her parents *died*. She's been living with her aunt and uncle since she was ten. I told you all this weeks ago." He shook his head at Duncan's look of recognition. "Anyway, she doesn't talk about it much, but what she has told me makes it sound like it wasn't the best of homes for her. Not happy. I get the impression they ignored her unless they had no choice."

"Hey, that sounds better than the screaming matches at my house."

Scott took a long drink and shook his head before he answered. "I can't say whose life is worse. I think you both have had it kind of rough."

"Maybe you're right." He shrugged. "I didn't mean to wake you up. Go back to sleep." He gestured to the bed.

"Nah, I had to wake up anyway. I fell asleep reading for class so I need to finish the work."

"Yeah, passing the class might be a good idea."

Scott grabbed his book from the foot of the bed and sat at the desk. Maybe if he were sitting up, he'd be more likely to stay awake. Opening it up to the page he was last on, he started reading.

"It's kind of ironic," Duncan said, settling on his bed.

"What is?"

"She figures I'm the one with the perfect life, and of the three of us, you're probably the happiest."

Scott looked at Duncan over his shoulder for a few minutes, thinking about what he said. For once, Duncan was looking past himself. Maybe there was hope for him yet. "Yeah," he mumbled and went back to the book.

Chapter Eight

Jamie walked – no, more like stumbled – into her dorm room after a long day of classes and work. She was going to quit this job. It would kill her; she was going to die of absolute boredom. How could doing nothing be so exhausting? The only time it was interesting and fun was when people were buying books at the beginning of the semester – there was a bit of a rush the last week classes could be added or dropped while people scrambled with new schedules – but now no one came in whatsoever. Not even for a notebook. Why work at a bookstore when she was getting paid to sit around and not do her homework. She would much rather have her homework done than get paid minimum wage to do nothing.

She dropped her bag on the floor and let herself fall on her bed, moaning.

"Having a bad day?" Amy asked from her desk. Jamie moaned again. "Classes? Or work?"

"Is there a difference?" she asked, muffled by her blanket. She shifted to her side facing Amy and kicked her shoes off her feet.

"I saw something, and I thought about you," Amy said. She typed something into her computer. "Here it is. I'll print it out for you."

"What is it?" Jamie asked.

"A job on campus."

"I already have one. I'm not allowed to have more than one." She rolled her eyes at the rule. "Besides, I have a hard enough time keeping up with homework now."

"Just look at it." Amy stretched across the span of the room, not getting out of her chair. Jamie rolled to hang half off the bed, stretching too, not wanting to leave the bed. She snatched the paper and flopped back onto her pillows. "The school newspaper is looking for a weekly writer. Wow, that would be fantastic...and kind of perfect."

"I know. I figured you're an English major with whatever that business thing is stacked on to it, so this might be good for you." Amy shrugged. "If I'm wrong, just forget it."

Jamie rolled off the bed and tackled her roommate. "This is perfect!"

"Oomph! Okay! Great. I'm glad."

Pulling back she looked at the paper. "Wow, it's up to two hundred bucks an article! That's more than a month of work at the bookstore! This is amazing. Thank you!" She hugged her again. "I can do this, and it's on my own time as long as I get it done once a week and in time for edits. This works so much better." She wished she had seen this before. The bookstore was a good run, but she was over it, and this worked amazingly with her major.

"I'm glad I could help." Amy beamed. "Well, it seems I have just won the best roommate award." She smiled rubbing her fingernails against her shirt. Jamie rolled her eyes and went back to her bed.

"Maybe. Let's see what else you can pull out the rest of the year." She sat down, reading the job posting again. "I should go tell Scott and Duncan."

Amy turned around in her chair to rest her arm across the back. "Okay, I have to ask. Which one of them is it?"

"Which one of them is what?"

"Which one is the one you *like*? Scott. Or Duncan."

Well, that was a question.

"Duncan," she said automatically, though it felt weird to say. "He's attractive. Nice. And, his family seems amazing from the photos I've seen. Scott said his parents and siblings come to all the school functions." She shrugged.

"What about Scott?" Amy asked

"He's my best friend," Jamie answered quickly.

Amy groaned and laid her hand across her eyes. "Oh, no. You've stuck him in the friend zone! Don't do that; don't ever do that!" Amy let out a frustrated sigh

"I didn't stick him anywhere. What does that mean anyway?"

"The friend zone is when you won't even let someone have the chance at being more than just a friend, even if it's *obvious* to everyone else. I see you, and I hide around the corner and watch, and I think he likes you." Amy explained. "And...you like him. You're just too stuck on Duncan to realize it."

"Scott doesn't think of me like that."

Amy snorted. "See? You just can't see it. You're so comfortable with him you don't realize it's the *good* kind of comfortable."

It should be natural.

Scott had said that to her just a couple of days after they met when he'd been giving her a hard time about flirting with Duncan.

"No..." Jamie said, shaking her head. *Really? Could Amy be right?* "Scott is just...Scott. That's the way he is. He—"

"Yeah, that's just Scott when he's with *you*."

"Okay, fine. I'll let the friend zone walls come down. We'll see what happens."

"Good, because he likes you, and you should let him like you." Amy tapped her desk with her fingertip as she spoke, making her points. "He doesn't just like you. He cares about you." She turned away when she said the last part, her voice dropping. "There's a difference."

"How about you then? Do you like anyone?" Jamie asked, wondering if her roommate's sudden switch was her normal mood swing or something else.

"Nope. Sorry. I don't like anyone," Amy said in a singsong voice, turning to look at Jamie again. "We're talking about you, anyway."

Jamie rolled her eyes and flopped back on the bed. She took a minute to think about the list of homework and projects she had to finish before Thanksgiving. The thought of the holiday made her skin crawl. She would be going back to Florida, and she'd gotten accustomed to living without the doom and gloom of Aunt Jane and Uncle Tim hanging over her. "I have so much to do," she mumbled.

"Yeah, like Scott."

Jamie squeaked and threw her pillow at Amy. "No! That is *not* letting down the friend zone walls. That's something completely different!" Jamie put her hands on her eyes. "I can't believe you just said that, Amy."

"Well, I did and I'm not even sorry," she stated with an emphatic nod of her head, a smile in her voice.

"What am I going to do with you? I swear."

She rolled over so she was facing the wall. This wasn't doing her reading and her homework, but she couldn't deal with that at the moment. She couldn't deal with her roommate, who was still laughing. Jamie sighed. "I can't even function right now."

"And, why is that? School? Work? Or me?"

"All Three," Jamie said with a laugh. She rolled enough to retrieve her bag and went back to face the wall. "I'm going to be reading for class. You do whatever it is you're doing, and I'll get back to you later."

Amy laughed.

"I don't find this funny."

"Oh, but I do."

"Yeah, I kinda figured." She opened her bag, pulled out her anthropology book, turned to where they were supposed to be reading, and skimmed the pages.

Her phone buzzed and moved across the bedspread until she snatched it up to look at the screen. And she smiled.

> What are you doing?

> Smiling because now I don't have to do anthro

Why?

Because I'm talking to you.

Glad to be of service.

"Who is it? *Scott*?" Amy teased, dragging out his name.

"Don't you have homework?"

Amy laughed, and Jamie heard the crack of a book's spine as she opened her text.

I have a question…

42

LOL No, another question. I'm in the mood for a decent pizza.

I don't see a question.

It's implied. Let's go get a pizza at that place down the street… On me.

Okay, but I'm driving. Your little car scares me.

Whatever. Meet you at the truck in ten.

kk

I've got something to tell you, too.

Jamie twisted and rolled off the bed in one motion, shoved her feet into her sneakers, slid her phone into her back pocket, grabbed her coat and bag, and was halfway to the door before Amy registered her leaving.

"Where are you going?"

"Out, Mom," Jamie said, exaggerating a whine.

"With who?"

"Scott. Don't. Say. A. Word."

Amy twisted her fingers in front of her mouth like she was locking her lips, but her smirk was undeniable. Her roommate's laughter carried into the hall through the closed door as Jamie left.

Whatever. Meet you at the truck in ten.

kk

I've got something to tell you, too.

SCOTT LOCKED HIS PHONE, POCKETED IT, AND RUMMAGED THROUGH HIS desk to find his wallet. It wasn't where he thought he left it. He could have sworn that it was in the top drawer, not the third one down. He must have been out of it when he came back the other night. He has found it in weirder places.

"Where are you going?" Duncan asked, turning in his chair.

"Out," Scott responded. He really didn't want Duncan coming along.

"Where is out?" *Oh God, he was pushing.*

"Pizza place down the street," he answered.

"Alone?" He let out a sigh.

"No, I'm going with Jamie." Duncan nodded and closed his computer, standing to his feet. "What are you doing?"

"I'll tag along. This will give me a chance to get in her good graces." Scott had the urge to smack him.

"She had something she wanted to tell me," he said, hoping the vague statement would discourage him enough to not come. But, he put on his jacket.

"Are you two dating?" Duncan asked.

"No."

"Then, there is no harm in me coming along." He smiled. "Meeting her at her truck, right?"

"Yeah," he nearly hissed.

The walk to the truck was silent. Oh, how he wanted to cast away Duncan with some magic power like in books and movies. But instead, he was stuck walking next to him to Jamie's truck.

"Oh hey, Duncan. I wasn't expecting you," Jamie called out as they neared the truck in the parking lot near her dorm.

"I couldn't pass up the chance." He smiled.

That smile ticked off Scott because he knew Jamie was melting in it.

"Yeah, no, it's chill," she said. "Get in. Let's go." Scott moved fast to get into the center seat of the truck. No way was he going to let Duncan get that. Was he going over the top? Nope, he didn't think so.

Once they were driving, Scott asked, "So, what was it you wanted to tell me?"

"Nope." She laughed. "You aren't going to get it out of me early. Let's get there and order first. It won't be that long. We're just around the corner from the place."

There was silence from that point on until they reached Mario's, home of the best pizza they'd found within a ten-mile radius of the school. Scott and Duncan sat on one side of the booth and Jamie on the other side.

"I'm going to use the restroom, I'll be right back," Jamie said, sliding out of the booth again.

Scott nodded and when she was out of range he turned to Duncan. "Why are you here?"

"I told you. To get in her good graces."

"She likes you as it is. Please, just let me have a meal with my friend, okay?"

Duncan clicked his tongue. "That might be hard. I mean you said she likes me. Well, who wouldn't, but still I need to scope out the situation."

Scott scoffed when the waitress walked up to the table. "Can I take your order?"

"One large cheese pizza, deep dish, a Coke for me," Duncan ordered.

"A Dr. Pepper for me and fifty/fifty mix of Coke and Dr. Pepper for Jamie."

The woman nodded and smiled at Scott. "The usual, huh? I will have that to you as soon as it's ready"

"Thank you." Scott turned to Duncan. "Tell me something, Duncan, did you know what I ordered is her favorite drink?"

"I do now," Duncan said with a smug smirk. "What did you order?"

"What did I miss?" Jamie asked, sliding back into the booth.

"Nothing. We ordered. I got your drink."

"Half and half?" she asked a smile pulling at her lips. Scott nodded. "I love you." Scott tried hard not to grin like an idiot, even though he knew she was kidding. "Okay, so my news then." She bounced in the seat, folding her hands on the table. "I found out the school paper is looking for an editor. It pays well, and I'm thinking about leaving the bookstore for it."

"That is perfect for you," Scott exclaimed.

'Why would you leave the bookstore?" Duncan asked, shrugging. "You're being paid to do nothing."

"That's the thing. I want to *do* something. Even if it means being paid by the article, I would feel like I'm doing something rather than setting aside hours a week to do nothing when I could be doing homework or something," she explained.

Scott clenched his teeth to keep from telling Duncan to shut up. If he kept it up, he was going to make her second guess herself.

"Jamie, this is the *perfect* job for you, and you know that," Scott encouraged

"Perfect or not, you shouldn't pass off the piece-of-cake job you have now."

"I need more *time*. This new job would help me out with that a lot because I would do it when I wanted, not when I was scheduled. I would be writing an article a week, too."

"I don't get it, but do what you think is right," Duncan said, dismissing her choice.

"Do what you feel is *right*," Scott said, glaring at Duncan.

"I have to think about it, I guess."

"Okay, I have a Coke, a Dr. Pepper, and a mix," the waitress said as she came back. Jamie smiled at her and then at Scott.

Scott smiled back.

"DOCTOR BOND! DOCTOR BOND! DOCTOR BOND!" JAMIE YELLED running down the hall to his office door she was very glad was open. She gripped her hands on the doorframe to stop herself from sliding right past his office. "Doctor Bond!"

He was halfway out of his chair, panic on his face. "Good lord, Jamie. What's wrong?"

She laughed even though she was out of breath. "Nothing. I have something I want to tell you."

His panic eased, though he was still blanched, and he smiled. He laid his palm against his chest and huffed. "You are likely to give me a heart attack, Miss Boyer. Come sit down and tell me then." He eased back down into his chair as she sat across from him, her leg bouncing. "Okay, what is it?"

"I applied for a position in the newspaper, and I *got* it. I now write for the school newspaper. A weekly article!"

"That's fantastic, Jamie," he declared, his smile spreading wide. "What about your job at the bookstore?" he asked putting his glasses on the desk.

"I quit the job," she said with a shake of her head and a shrug. "I hated it, and the newspaper pays more per article than I get in a month through the store."

"I'm happy to see *you* so happy. You deserve to be happy."

"I can *be* happy, Doctor Bond. I just don't like to put it 'out there' for everyone else to see."

"Why is that, do you think?"

She sighed and slumped into her chair. Jamie shrugged. At first, she didn't like how he made her analyze herself to answer his questions, but she'd gotten used to it. It was easier all the time. "Because... well, because I shouldn't have to."

"You shouldn't have to show you're happy?"

"No...I mean I shouldn't have to be obvious about it. If someone knows me, and cares enough to know me, then they'll know how I feel."

He nodded. "I see. But, if you hide how you feel then how *is* someone supposed to learn who you are? To learn how to know you?"

"Why do you always ask me such tough questions?" she asked with a laugh and crossed her arms over her body.

"Because I care about you and want to learn about you," he said with a wink, throwing her own words right back at her.

Jamie leaned forward and took a handful of M&Ms from a dish on his desk, popping them in her mouth before she sat back, giving herself a few minutes to think about his question. She hadn't ever felt the need to hide anything from Doctor Bond, which was different. Since her parents died she'd learned to put on a good face, act a part, and play a role in her guardian's play of sympathy.

And, in that, she found her answer.

"I've had to fake it for so long, sometimes I don't know for sure what it is I feel. So, if I'm not sure, how can anyone else be?"

"But, you know you're happy." She nodded and he smiled, tapping his fingers on the desk blotter. "Good. I'm glad I've earned the privilege to see you happy. I wonder what I did to deserve it."

"The second time you ever saw me you knew I was messed up. No one has ever broken me like that."

"My intention wasn't to break you," he said, his voice softer.

"I don't mean *break* in a bad way. I mean you figured me out. You got me to talk. And cry. I hadn't cried in years." Just talking about it made her throat tighten. Jamie huffed and threw out her arms. "And, here I am." She smiled and stood up, going to a section of the wall where he had several diplomas and certificates hanging. "I like your office. Kinda small, but I like it."

"It's quaint."

"Doctor Bond, quaint is bigger than this. This is just small." She heard his chuckle behind her. "University of Cambridge, huh? Are you British, or did you pick up the accent while you were there?"

"I don't have an accent..." Jamie looked over her shoulder at him and raised an eyebrow. He laughed, a deep, rumbling sound. "Okay, fine. I have an accent. No, I am not British, but I lived in England from the time I was about twelve. My father worked overseas, so I spent much of my formative years there. I moved back to New York after university."

"I think I get smarter just talking to you, Doctor Bond." She finished her short stroll halfway around his office, then sat again, taking another handful of candy.

Doctor Bond watched her for a few moments, bouncing the eraser end of his pencil in the palm of his other hand. "Jamie, how are you doing otherwise?" he asked. "Have you said anything to your aunt and uncle about the letter? Or their trip?"

She shook her head. "Nothing to say about it, and saying something will just start a fight I don't have the energy for." She shrugged. "Granted, all they've done to contact me since I left Florida is three text messages, each one angrier than the last because I haven't answered. I'll respond tonight and act like I forgot my phone went off," she explained.

"You could do that. Or you could talk to them."

"No." She shook her head. "No, I can't talk to them. Not yet. It still hurts." His eyes pinched at the corner, and she shook her head again. "It just hurts, Doctor Bond. Here." She put her hand on her chest. "But, it's not enough to make me do anything stupid. I don't have to." He raised an eyebrow. Doctor Bond could say more with a facial expression than most said with a ten-minute speech. "I'm not dealing with it alone."

"No, you're not." He nodded. "You're going to talk to them eventually."

"I'm going back to Florida for Thanksgiving. I guess I'll have to talk to them then." She sighed. "When I do talk to them, it's not going to be for me. It'll be for you because there is no way I'm doing it for any other reason."

"Thank you, but I ask for you. Not me."

As much as he could ask her a question with a raise of his eyebrows, or encourage her with a smile, Jamie thought she saw something else in his eyes that day. She hadn't ever been one to believe eyes could tell all that much, or change to match a person's emotions, but if they did then she thought she saw it today. His eyes looked grayer than usual, pinched more, just sad. "What about you, Doctor Bond? How are you?"

"Is it your turn to make me talk then?" he said with a smile, but he didn't look at her when he did it, and the smile was less than convincing.

"Guess so. Turn around is fair play."

He picked up his glasses and tapped the bow against the desk, slowly, rhythmically. "It has been a very hard week."

"Why?" She leaned back in her chair.

"Two years ago on Saturday, we lost Rachel."

Jamie fell silent, and for a moment she empathized with all the people who had ever said to her "I don't know what to say," when they heard about her parents.

Finally, she swallowed and whispered, "I'm so sorry."

"Thank you," he said with a heavy sigh and looked around the room. His smile was there, still strained, but better. "I would show you a photo, but I took it home to get a new frame for it."

Jamie swallowed before she was able to ask, "How old was she?"

"She was eleven, she'd be thirteen now." Then he looked at her. "There won't be a class on Friday."

"No, I totally understand. I'm sure the class will as well."

"I don't plan on telling the class, in truth. Some of the older students know about Rachel, they were in my class when it happened, and I had to take some time. Not many other people know about Rachel."

"Rachel is a pretty name..."

The smile flashed more genuine. "She was named after her grandmothers. Rachel was my mother's name, and Marie was my wife's mother."

"Are they both gone?" Jamie asked.

Doctor Bond nodded. "My wife and I are the only ones left. We were both only children." He gave a small shrug. "Perhaps one day we can have another child." He looked at his watch. "I have a class to teach in two minutes. Sorry to end this meeting short and on a sad note."

"It doesn't have to be a sad note. I like hearing about her." When Doctor Bond came around his desk to open the door for her, Jamie held her spot. He stopped his hand on the knob, looking at her. "Doctor Bond, may I give you a hug?" she asked with a smile, teasing him with a reminder of the first time they'd talked.

Then his smile was real and he nodded and she gave him a quick squeeze before he opened the door and they left together.

Jamie sat in class her legs kicked up on the chair and her back against the wall. She was happy for once. It seemed like the days she wasn't happy were few and far between. Waiting for Scott to show up to class, she was on her iPhone looking through Facebook and Tumblr when a text message popped up. She accidentally pressing on it when she went to look at her notifications, and saw Scott was the one to send it.

Sick as a dog. Tell Bond I won't be in class today.

Feel better!

The power went out as she put her phone down on the table. The entirety of the room fell silent. Then everything dropped. Jamie clutched onto the desk as her body lifted from her chair. She screamed, but the sound was lost in the free fall. She felt like she was on the Tower of Terror in DisneyWorld. Whatever the room hit to make it stop, it hit hard. Jamie slammed against the table, pain shooting through her when her shoulder cracked. Looking around, there was no one else though she was sure the class was nearly full when they fell.

A sound brought her back to reality. A low growl. She looked in the direction that she thought the sound was coming from. Doctor Bond!

He was on his back with piles of trash and metal on top of him. Jamie ran to his side, pushing off all the trash she could. She saw blood. A lot of it. No, no that is not good.

"Doctor Bond," she whispered, digging her pocket and pulling out some tissues to wipe the blood away from his eyes. "Doctor Bond, please be all right."

"Jamie," he whispered in a rough, hoarse voice. "I...I don't think I can."

"You don't think you can what?" she asked. "Please stay awake."

"I don't think I can." His body was still.

Jamie shook her head.

"No, Doctor Bond," she begged, tears burning her eyes. "You are like my dad. I haven't had a dad in such a long time. Please, Doctor Bond, don't go. Don't leave me!"

"You can do it, Jamie. You can be strong."

JAMIE SAT UP IN HER BED, GASPING FOR BREATH. THE CLOCK BY HER head read four in the morning. Running her hands over her face, she realized she had been crying. That dream hurt. Hurt a lot more than it should have. It was just a dream

No, no way it could ever happen.

None.

Chapter Nine

Jamie sat in the hallway outside anthropology, reading a book before class started in another ten minutes. She wanted to escape the dark images stealing her sleep. It was getting bad. She would wake up in a cold sweat and need to do something – anything – to get her mind off the dream. Too bad most of the time when she woke up it was two or three in the morning. Not much she could do in the wee hours before she needed to be up, and without waking up Amy. So she would normally sneak into the bath and do something benign like wash her face or braid her hair.

She figured facials were better than most of the alternatives she could have come up with, and she'd be lying if anyone asked her if she wanted to do something other than excessive personal hygiene, and she said no. She got so tired, so frustrated, she wanted to hit the wall or rage and scream, but she didn't. She promised Doctor Bond she wasn't going to hurt herself or do anything stupid. She'd promised him she'd text him when she felt out of control, and she already had about the dreams and what she was doing to shake them off. Her face had never been cleaner.

A shadow loomed over her. Looking up at Scott, Jamie dog-eared the page and tapped the floor next to her for him to sit. "Hey, there. When did you get back?" She closed the book and put it in her bag.

Scott sat down next to her, his knee bumping hers as he settled, a wide smile on his face. "Late last night. I figured you were asleep, or I would have texted."

If only...

"Did your sister have a good birthday?"

"Yeah. Looked like she did anyway. Mom threw the party, and Dad took her and her friends to the movies and ice cream after."

Jamie found herself smiling back at his contagious grin. "You look happy."

He smiled wider, and she noticed for the first time he had a dimple to the right of his chin when he smiled. "I am."

"Well, are you going to tell me why?" she asked, rolling her eyes. She nudged him with a small shove of her shoulder against his.

"I just am. Can't I be happy?" He reached into his bag and pulled out a small brown, purple, and gold gift bag. "We went into the city on Saturday, and I got these for you."

"And what are these?" She took the bag, her curiosity piqued. Opening the bag she peeked inside, the delicious scent of cocoa filling her nose. "Chocolate? This is perfect!" She took out the package inside, a clear plastic box filled with an assortment of multi-colored candies and chocolates. The box said Koppers Chocolate. Jamie worked to open the box and popped one into her mouth before showing him the box. The candy coating gave way to a creamy, sweet, chocolate center with a hint of something fruity, like pomegranate. "Oh, wow. These are delicious. Have one." She held the box out to him.

"No, I got it for you."

"Come on, Take a piece." She shoved the box under his nose. When he still didn't take one, she picked a random piece and held it to his mouth until he grinned and opened his mouth and took the candy from her fingers.

He grinned and chewed.

"So why did you feel the need to get me chocolate?" she asked, looking through the box for the next one she was going to eat.

"Can't I buy you a box of chocolate for no reason?"

"Sure, it could happen but when I get an answer like *that*, there's a reason." She found one she wanted and popped it into her mouth. Covering her mouth with one hand, she spoke again "So what is it?"

"I saw the box, and you're a chocolate person, so I got it." Jamie chewed her chocolate staring at him. "Not going for it?" he asked with arched eyebrows beneath his dark hair. Jamie shook her head. Scott shrugged and took a candy from the box. "Too bad because that's what happened."

Jamie rolled her eyes and swallowed the candy. "I suppose I have to learn to live with that lie." She smiled

"Yeah, you're going to have to."

"Ha! So it *was* a lie!"

"I'm neither confirming nor denying the accusation."

Jamie narrowed her eyes. Oh yeah, that was a lie, A complete and total lie. Another shadow hovered over them. Jamie looked up to Doctor Bond.

"Hi, there." She held the box of Kopper's Chocolates over her head. "Want a chocolate?" she asked holding the box up to him.

Smiling, Doctor Bond took a chocolate. "I love Kopper's Chocolates. My favorites are the sea salt caramels." He took another two candies before putting one in his mouth. "Why are you sitting out here? There are seats inside."

"I felt the need to sit on the floor. And, I think it's weird to be alone in a classroom." She shrugged. Scott stood and offered her his hand to draw her to her feet. "I was reading, then Scott came by. With chocolate."

Doctor Bond smiled at Scott and motioned toward the door. "Well, come into the room. I'm sure the chair is far better than the hard floor."

"A hard chair in replacement to the hard floor?" Scott murmured.

"Might be a little bit better for your back," he said over his shoulder as he walked into the room, Jamie following him and Scott behind her. The two of them went to their normal seats. "So what have the two of you been up to?" he asked, putting his bag down, and clapping his hands against the podium. "I take it you went home, Mr. Scotch?"

"For the weekend, yeah. My sister's thirteenth birthday."

Jamie looked at Doctor Bond, a cold lump hitting her stomach where the chocolate sat. Scott had no way of knowing the professor's only daughter would be thirteen. It was a coincidence, but her heart immediately hurt for him.

"That's great." Doctor Bond looked at her, scrutinizing. Then he tipped up his chin. "And you? How are you?"

His tone said a whole heck of a lot more than his words. Jamie swallowed and shrugged, sliding a glance at Scott. "Oh, you know. Same old, same old. I've been reading this cheesy romance book. I was expecting some angst, but that doesn't seem to be happening."

Doctor Bond gave a small laugh and rubbed his eyes with one hand. "Well, I'm sure that it will come soon. After all, doesn't every romance have angst?"

"Doctor Bond, are you feeling alright?" He seemed too tight, too tense, something. Not his normal, energetic, enthusiastic self.

"Getting a bit of a cold. It's nothing to worry about." He waved it off as students started to walk into the room. "I'll be fine, Jamie."

Jamie gave a small nod and sat down in her chair. Watching him. Then she caught Scott studying her the same way. She smiled at Scott, putting the box of chocolates between them.

"Let's eat these before my roommate knows about them." She smiled, taking one from the box and biting into it. Scott took another. The class went quickly, mostly because she found anthropology interesting. Doctor Bond coughed a few times and definitely wasn't as animated as usual, but he said it was just the start of a cold.

Class was dismissed. Waving to Doctor Bond as she left she pulled around the corner where Scott waited for her.

"I want to talk to you about something," Scott said, taking her elbow to pull her closer to the wall and out of the line of human traffic.

Jamie nodded. "Alright." She pulled the bag closer to herself. "What's up?"

"Are you okay?" he asked. "I'm worried about you."

"There's nothing to worry about," she said quickly, turning away, but his hand on her elbow stopped her again.

"I think there is, Jamie. I don't think you're sleeping."

She spun and stared at him, her jaw hanging. "How do – how could you know that? I didn't tell—"

Scott stepped closer and she had to tip her head to keep looking in his face. "Your eyes are shadowed, you act tired, you're yawning a lot..." He smiled, but it was an odd smile. "Although, your skin looks amazing."

"You pay too much attention to stuff that you don't need to worry about."

"I don't think so," he said with a shake of his head. "I think I'm paying attention to all the right things and if I want to worry, I'll worry." She stared at him, trying to figure out how to process his questions. Scott drew in a breath and reached for her hand, the one with the still red and puckered burn scar, and held it up as if presenting the scar, then into her eyes again. "Jamie, when you burned your hand you told me you weren't paying attention."

"Yeah..."

Scott sighed. "I have a confession to make."

"Conversations beginning with 'I have a confession' are always interesting—"

He kept going as if she'd said nothing. "That day, when you stayed behind to talk to Doctor Bond...I waited outside the door, Jamie."

She gasped. "You listened to what we were talking about?" Scott nodded, but she shook her head. "I told you not to wait, to just go ahead." She pinched the bridge of her nose. "He said he thought you'd be waiting," she mumbled, then faced Scott again. "You weren't out here when I left the room."

"No, I wasn't. I didn't listen to everything." He shook his head. "I couldn't process the little I heard, but I heard enough. I know you did it on purpose, it wasn't an accident, and you weren't just distracted."

"Scott, you don't have to worry—"

"Jamie, I'm worried about you because you are worth more than that."

She shook her head. "Scott, please stop."

"I don't know what I'm supposed to do to help; just tell me, and I will do it." He turned her hand so he was holding it instead.

"I'm fine." Jamie swallowed and drew in a fortifying breath. Doctor Bond had told her he believed Scott would be there for her, as much as he was. She trusted him, trusted his judgment, so maybe she *could* trust Scott. Jamie took a step closer to Scott so what she said would be for him only. "You're right, I did burn myself on purpose that day."

"Because of the letter?"

"You remember?"

He nodded. "Of course I do."

Something warm bloomed in Jamie's chest, pleasant and comfortable. She smiled, not even sure why. "That night I was just...I couldn't think straight. But, Scott, please believe me it was the first time. And the last time."

"Do you swear that to me?"

"I swear."

"But you're not sleeping..."

"I sleep. Some. But I'm not awake doing something stupid. I'm just...awake." He didn't look convinced. Jamie chuckled and slid her arms around him, pressing her cheek to his chest. Scott immediately wrapped her in an embrace, resting his chin on top of her head. "I'm fine, I swear. Thank you." She pulled away and smiled. "Is this what the chocolate was for? An interrogation tool? Maybe I would talk if I had chocolate in me?" She chuckled.

Scott shrugged, his hand rubbing a small spot on her back. "That may have crossed my mind, but honestly, I saw the chocolate and thought of you. I don't think you minded."

"No, I guess I didn't mind."

"I'm still going to worry."

Jamie rolled her eyes and nudged him with her shoulder. "Yes, you'd better worry about being late to your study session for English."

Scott looked at his watch. "Crap, you're right. I will talk to you later. I'll text you," he called over his shoulder as he jogged away.

Jamie chuckled and bent over to pick up her bag. Something caught her attention and she looked back to the anthropology classroom door. Doctor Bond stood in the doorway, his shoulder leaning into the jamb. When she met his eyes, he smiled and winked and disappeared back through the door.

Jamie sat in Doctor Bond's office sideways in the chair resting her legs over the chair so the arm was under her kneecaps. She dropped her head back and let out a bored sigh. Something bounced on her stomach.

"What was that?" She looked around trying to find what hit her.

"Something to keep you entertained," Doctor Bond said, going back to the open book and notebook on his desk.

Jamie twisted until she could lean over the side of the chair and retrieve a yellow ball with a smiley face. "Was it this?" She picked up the stress ball under her chair.

Doctor Bond looked at her over his glasses and nodded, doing a rotten job of hiding his smirk. Jamie went back to her original position and threw the ball up in the air, catching it as it came down. She caught it and looked to Doctor Bond, who was fully engrossed again in his reading. She looked at the ball, smiled, and threw it at him. It bounced off his curly hair. Jamie quickly clasped her hands together twiddling her thumbs but failed miserably at whistling.

"My intent in giving it to you wasn't to have you bound it off my head."

Jamie looked at him with wide eyes. "Do what?" she asked, shrugging. Then she looked around. "Hey, where did that stress ball go?" she asked, looking at the ground, acting like she was looking for it.

She knew it had rolled under his desk, but she wasn't going to be the one to find it.

"You are just like my daughter," he said with a chuckle and smile. "Stop it." The ball came rolling from under the desk. He must have kicked it.

"Is that a 'Stop it, you're a pest' kind of stop it, or 'You remind me of my daughter and I don't want you to' kind of stop it?" she asked. "I don't want to be a bother, but if I am, I'll leave." She sat properly in the chair folding her hands in her lap, the stress ball forgotten for the moment.

"You are *not* a bother, at least not enough of one I want you to leave," he said, his smile making her feel better. "And as far as reminding me of Rachel, that's a good thing. Remembering doesn't hurt, not in any way I want to stop."

He set down his pen and took hold of a small silver frame to the left side of his desk, handing it to her. The photo was of a girl maybe nine or ten years old. Blond hair cascaded down her back and a pair of vibrant blue eyes looked back at whoever had taken the picture, a wide smile much like her father's curved her lips. It was autumn and leaves were on the ground adding yellow, brown, and red undertones to the photo.

"She's beautiful," Jamie managed to say with her voice level, passing back the photo. "I wish I could have met her. Sounds like we might have gotten along."

"She got along with everyone, once we got her to talk to people. She was very shy. But once she opened up, then she acted much like you. Much the same humor." He looked away and chuckled, and Jamie figured he might be remembering something. She stayed silent not wanting to disturb the happy memories. Then his smile slid a little and he touched the photo. "She was the light of my life."

"Was it a surprise when she passed?" she asked, leaning down to pick the ball up that was against her foot. She fiddled with it in her hands, bouncing it back and forth.

"It was," he said with a nod, turning his attention back to her. "Completely. She fell ill on a Thursday and was gone by Saturday. We never had any idea she had the condition. Nothing pointed to it. She was healthy, not even allergies, and with the family history we were very careful." He shook his head. "I knew what to look for, and I never saw it."

Jamie tilted her head to the side. "You knew what to look for?"

"Her condition was genetic." A pained pinch pulled at his eyes. "From me. Hypertrophic Cardiomyopathy. Except I knew about mine since I was much younger, just a toddler." He removed his reading glasses and folded his hands under his chin.

Jamie's eyes widened. "You have what killed her?"

"Yes, but as I said, I've known most of my life. Rachel's form of the disease had a rapid onset and no previous indications." Apparently, she had a look of shock on her face, because he held up a hand and shook his head, smiling. "Don't look at me like that, I'm not going anywhere. Honestly. I plan on seeing *you* graduate, get married, and have children."

"You can be grandpa," she said with a laugh, even though her chest ached with it all. He would never be a real grandfather because his daughter was gone; Jamie's children would never have grandparents because her parents were gone. The whole thing sucked. "You'd be better than Aunt Jane and Uncle Tim. They didn't want kids to begin with."

"You know, there's a name for your aunt and uncle."

"Oh, I can think of a few..."

"No, I mean D.I.N.K. Stands for double-income-no-kids."

"Yeah, that's about right." Jamie sighed. "I can remember when I was younger, before Mom and Dad were gone, Aunt Jane and Uncle Tim came over a lot. I always wondered about why they didn't have kids. They were older than my parents; Aunt Jane was my mother's sister. Mom told me Aunt Jane and Uncle Tim liked being just Aunt Jane and Uncle Tim." She shrugged. "Guess I messed up their plans."

"I don't understand why they took you as your guardians if their heart wasn't in it."

She shrugged again. "The funny thing is I loved them so much before. They always seemed happy to come, and Aunt Jane would play games with me. We had fun. When I found out I was going to live with them, I thought it would be okay." Jamie realized tears had slipped free, and she swiped at them, looking down. "'What would we be if we didn't take her in?'" she repeated, mocking her aunt's voice.

"Their choice was the right one, Jamie. But, I don't believe they made it for the right reasons."

"Maybe they did it for the money," she said with a wry, humorless laugh. "Surprise! All they could do with my parent's estate other than sell the house. Everything else was left to me. I haven't done anything but go to college off of it. And buy my truck."

"What do you mean?"

"My parents weren't wealthy, I mean not stinkin' rich or anything, but they made sure if anything ever happened I'd be taken care of. My aunt and uncle were my guardians, but the money was mine when I turned eighteen. I decided to use it for college."

She couldn't decide where she wanted to look, at Doctor Bond or the floor. Was she even allowed to talk about how much money she had?

"That was a good decision." He nodded.

"I've talked with the man who set up the trust. My parents trusted him, so I guess I do, too. I can get my doctorate and still have plenty of money left over."

Doctor Bond put his glasses back on and picked up his pen. "I haven't given you nearly enough credit, Miss Boyer," he said, ribbing her by being formal. It was a joke between them. "Use it for a top-notch education. Don't let anyone change your mind." He nodded to himself. "Speaking of education, I need to finish this for class."

Jamie nodded and stood up.

"No problem. I'll see you in class." She smiled, placed the stress ball on the table, and walked out of the room. Once she reached the doorframe she felt something hit the back of her head. Shaking her head, she smiled and kept walking.

JAMIE STRETCHED OUT ON THE FLOOR OF SCOTT AND DUNCAN'S ROOM on her back, her backside against the wall and her legs folded as if she were sitting on the floor, her English book balanced on her stomach with her anthropology book next to her, the next thing to tackle before she went back to her dorm. Duncan was at his desk, his fingers tapping away on his computer, and Scott sat on the floor, just past her head, his back against the side of his bed. The three of them were silent, doing their own thing. Any time the boys' dorm was open Jamie was there. It was quiet, calm, and drama-free.

Usually.

"You know you need to have both feet on the ground," a voice coming from the doorway broke the silence.

"Give it a break, Thad," Duncan mumbled, not even looking up from his computer. "Clearly the majority of her person is on the floor."

Jamie laid the book face down on her chest and twisted her head so she could see past Scott's legs to watch. By what she could tell looking at him upside down, the speaker was a tall, skinny kid with bushy-curly hair and a bad case of acne. He stood in the doorway with his arms crossed, scowling at them.

"But the rules say—"

"Does it look like we care what the rules say?" Scott said, shaking his head. "No one is breaking any rules, Thad."

"Look, I just don't want you to get in trouble."

"Yeah, right," Duncan mumbled.

"We aren't going to," Scott practically growled, setting his pencil in the binding of his book before he looked up again. "I mean, look at her. She *was* reading, but now she's watching us argue over nothing."

"What's the fighting all about?" a third voice called from somewhere down the hall.

"It's Steven, the RA," Scott said, looking down at her. He set his hand on her shoulder. "Jamie, don't move, we need him to see how you are sitting."

Holding up her thumb, she twisted it so it was a thumbs up for them.

"Steven, I'm just reminding them that girls have to have both feet on the ground at all times," Thad said, looking smug.

"Wow, is he the hall monitor of the week?" Jamie asked.

Scott chuckled and smiled down at her.

A red-haired kid walked around the corner, and even though she was kind of looking at him upside down and sideways, she recognized him. The hair was hard to forget. "Hey, I know you!" Jamie said pointing at him. "You helped me move into my dorm on the first day."

"Hey, Ahh, Jamie, right?" he asked leaning against the doorframe opposite Thad.

"That's correct." She smiled at him, not moving from how she was. If she swung around to stand, she'd probably topple over dizzy. "Are you the RA?" she asked, trying to tilt her head so she could see not completely upside-down.

"I am indeed. I didn't know you came up on this floor." He stroked what little red facial hair he had.

"Every open hours." She smiled. "Neither of these two have kicked me out yet, so I just keep coming."

"Steven, the *feet*." Thad motioned toward them.

"What is with him?" she mumbled again to Scott.

Steven kept stroking his facial hair, what pathetic little there was of it. "Thad, the guideline is for *other* situations. She's doing homework. So is Scott. They aren't alone. The door is open for anyone and everyone to see. If they were in a compromising position, I'd worry, but I'm not." He pointed back and forth between her and Scott. "But keep the rules in mind. No funny business."

Jamie nodded and gave him a thumbs up, too, which was more of a thumbs down from her angle. She snorted a laugh and twisted her hand so her thumb pointed to the ceiling. "Got it," she said with faked enthusiasm.

"Hey, why isn't anyone worried about me?" Duncan said, twisting in his chair. "Maybe I'm the one you need to warn about funny business."

"Seriously?" Scott said and threw his pen at Duncan.

"Thanks, Steven! It was good to see you again!" Jamie yelled as the RA walked away.

"Sorry, Thad. No excitement tonight," Scott said, and Thad walked away huffing.

"Why did he want us to get in trouble so bad?" Jamie asked, tilting her head so she was now looking at both Scott and Duncan.

"He was the last one to do the walk of shame," Duncan explained. "And until the next one happens he gets ragged on."

"Walk of shame?" she asked. "I mean, I know what *walk of shame* usually means, but..."

"Let's just call it a *preventative* walk of shame. If you get caught breaking the rules, you get escorted from the dorm. Loudly. Publicly. Everyone lines the halls and there are no rules. You get stuff thrown at you, people yelling, teasing, wolf-whistling, the works. They pull out the Nerf guns, silly string, confetti, you name it. It's *not* fun," Scott explained, shaking his head

Jamie squinted at him. "Have *you* done the walk of shame?"

Scott looked shocked. "With who? You're the only girl I...you're the only girl who ever comes up here. And you're gone before the end of open hours. That's when it happens."

Now, Jamie was curious. "So what...you walk out and you get yelled at by the people on the floor?"

"Oh, worse than that," Duncan said. "The worst I have seen was when Derek took chocolate sauce and put it in that one chick's hair. Man, what was her name."

"Amy," Scott said, looked down at Jamie, and winked.

Jamie's jaw fell open. "Are you kidding me?" Scott shook his head and Jamie started laughing. "Oh, my gosh. That's why she came in ticked off that one night."

"What do you mean?" Duncan asked, rotating in his chair.

"Amy is her roommate," Scott explained.

"Yeah, and a few weeks ago she came into the room flat out pissed and I couldn't get her to talk about it. That's why. She had chocolate sauce in her hair!" Jamie couldn't help but laugh some more.

"She *would* be *your* roommate," Duncan said.

"What does that mean?"

"It means that you *never* get in trouble. How often is she in trouble?"

Jamie tapped her chin. "I don't know. I don't start out conversations with, 'hey how was your day? Did you get in trouble?' If I did then there are bigger issues that needed to be worked out." She smiled as she saw Duncan roll his eyes. "Don't roll your eyes at me, young man," she scolded, pointing at him. "Do your homework!"

"I'm sick of counting isotopes," he said, twisting back in his chair.

"You are the one who wanted to be the doctor, so don't complain." She picked her English back up from her chest. "I just want to write."

Chapter Ten

JAMIE LEANED AGAINST THE DOORFRAME, BITING HER LOWER LIP TO KEEP from laughing. She had been standing there for several minutes watching Duncan and Scott working silently and diligently on their homework. Each sat at their own desks, heads down, backs to each other. Scott was closest at his desk, and Duncan on the other side of the room. Scott turned a page, tipping his head to the left to keep reading.

She cleared her voice, and both of them jump. "Can I sit down, or am I just supposed to stand out here all evening?"

She liked surprising them and found it interesting to watch them when they didn't know she was watching them. Maybe Doctor Bond was rubbing off on her in more ways than she realized. Duncan jumped and cursed, just twisting in his chair to scowl at her, but Scott stood.

"Language, Mr. Buchanan," Jamie said, clicking her tongue.

"Sit at my desk," Scott said, scooping up his notebook and book from the desk and moving to his bed, sitting cross-legged facing the desk.

Jamie sat at his desk, spinning in the chair so she could see both of them. Duncan had gone back to studying, but Scott had set his book and notebook aside, watching her.

"What are you doing for Thanksgiving?" Jamie asked in general.

"Do we have options?" Duncan said, not lifting his head. "I'm going home to deal with The Face" He finally turned enough to look at her and offered a shrug. "I'll be back here as soon as I can. Trust me."

Jamie was going to say something, but Scott answered her question, too.

"Yeah, going home. Mom starts cooking on Monday, and I think we eat for three days straight. We start with Chinese Takeout Wednesday night and eat until every piece of pie is gone." He was smiling until he glanced at her. She wondered what he saw when he looked at her that made his smile slip. "What about you, Jamie?" he asked.

Jamie bit her lip and got up from the chair to sit on the edge of Scott's bed near the end, being sure to keep her two feet on the floor in case Thad went by. *The pain in the backside.* She sighed and looked down at her hands, picking at a frayed cubicle. "I'm going back to Florida. I'd rather not, but I need to talk to Aunt Jane and Uncle Tim before they leave for their long vacation." She looked at Scott, who was still watching her, his smile gone. "I've got some things to deal with." Scott nodded, just a single top of his head. She looked at Duncan. "The Face?"

"It's what I call my mother," he answered, sitting up straight to turn and face them, hanging his arm over the back of the chair. "She always has to put on her 'face' for people." His phone buzzed and shimmied across his desk. "Speak of the devil, she's calling me now." Duncan stood and picked up the phone.

Jamie scowled, watching him go. She couldn't make out what he said, but the tone of his voice was easy to read. Jamie turned to Scott, not saying word.

Scott shifted forward, talking lower so she could hear him but their voices wouldn't carry out to Duncan. "He tries to hide how broken his family really is."

"But his parents are married..."

"Doesn't mean they're happy. He doesn't say a whole lot about it but he's said enough I know the whole family pretends. In public, on the surface, nothing could be wrong. But I guess once the guests are gone and the door shuts behind them, the house becomes a war zone," Scott explained.

"I would never imagine any of that," she muttered.

"Yeah, because that's what he wants. He wants to be..." He trailed off, then shrugged. "Perfect."

Jamie shook her head. "But look at the photos." She gestured to the family photo Duncan had on his desk. "How can that be a war zone?"

"Ever watch the news, and they slide this heartwarming story in the middle of stories about war and crime? That's a heartwarming story in the middle of the chaos." He pointed to the same photo. "I would think you would understand."

"I do understand. I guess he's better at hiding it than I am."

"You hide it," Scott said, and she looked at him. "Except you can't hide from the people who care enough to know you."

She shrugged. "I guess I don't have enough patience, or acting skills, or whatever to pretend things are perfect. I mean, I *honestly* thought he had a near-perfect life." She waved her hand toward his picture.

A part of her hated the fact the main thing she thought she found appealing in him was his family. The nuclear family she'd lost, maybe.

"What is perfect, Jamie? There is no 'perfect' family," Scott said in an almost too calm voice. Not angry or upset, just level. "Perfect is what you make it. You can be happy without being perfect."

"Like your family?" she asked. "Your parents are divorced."

"Yeah, but that doesn't mean we're all miserable or anything. My parents got divorced when I was fifteen. My sister was ten. But, it wasn't like all the horror stories you hear. They just..." He shrugged. "They decided it was better to not be married than married. My dad will come by for Thanksgiving and bring Lois."

"Who's Lois?"

"My stepmother. They got married a few months ago."

"Do you like her?"

Scott smiled and shrugged one shoulder. "Sure. She's nice."

"So, everything is perfect."

Scott looked at her and smiled again. A different kind of smile, the kind of smile that always made her smile back. "No, but we're happy. So, it's good."

Jamie turned her head to glance at Duncan's desk. His 'perfect' was a fake perfect, too perfect. Was perfect supposed to be a general thing or did it have a definition? No, Scott was right. Perfect for her would be happy. Maybe perfect for someone else could be no fighting, but then perfect could be getting big, massive gifts for Christmas but not seeing their family often.

"You're right," Jamie admitted and focused on Scott again. "I'd rather have happy."

Scott squeezed her hand. She was surprised at how natural it felt.

Duncan walked back in, tapping off his phone. "What did I miss?"

"Nothing," both Jamie and Scott answered at the same time, then they both laughed at Duncan's confused look.

"You didn't miss anything," she said, shaking her head. "Just talking." Her bun loosened, and she reached over her head, quickly unbundling and re-twisting the hair like she had hundreds of times before. She didn't need a mirror and even knew how to maneuver the scrunchie so she never had to let go of the twist.

"Can I ask you a question?" Duncan asked.

"Is that the question?"

"Funny. Don't you ever take your hair out of the bun?"

"What sort of question is that?" she asked laughing again. He didn't answer, but crossed his arms, waiting. "Fine, I do when I go to sleep, But I'd rather have it in the bun. It's out of my face. It's long and gets in the way."

"How long is long?" Scott asked.

Jamie stood up and turned her back to him, reaching behind her to lay the flat of her hand against her back just above the waist of her jeans. "About here, lower back"

"Wow," Scott said. She thought she felt him touch her hand, but when she twisted and tried to see, his hands were in his lap.

"Take it down," Duncan ordered.

She scowled at him. "No."

"Come on. Let us see."

"No," she said, stepping closer to the door.

"Aww, come on," Duncan whined. "Scott wants to see, too."

She looked to Scott, but he didn't either deny or confirm Duncan's accusation.

"No, sorry." A smile crept across her face. "My hair has been in a bun for as long as I can remember. My mother used to put it up like this even when I was little."

"There's always room for change," Duncan tried.

"I'm not going to change because you want me to."

"Scott, help me out here," Duncan pleaded.

Jamie looked to Scott, waiting for him to side with his roommate. He met her gaze, then she shook her head. "Nah, it's her hair. She'll show it to who she wants to show it when she wants to show it." He looked at Duncan. "I'd drop it if I were you."

"That's right. I'm going to be accepted, my hair bun and all." She looked at Scott who gave a small smile. "I think I'm going to leave you to your homework. I'm going to do my own."

Jamie dreaded the entire drive home. She left campus at four in the morning on Monday and pulled into the driveway a little before midnight. She didn't plan on staying the whole week, or any longer than needed, and figured she'd leave the day after Thanksgiving to beat the worst of the traffic going back to campus. She even plotted out money to sleep in a hotel for the night on the way back, maybe somewhere around Virginia. She just had to make it through the next thirty-six hours or so.

The house was dark, quiet, and locked up when she turned off the truck. She unlocked the door, turned off the house alarm, and locked up behind her. The house was completely still, and for a minute she wondered if maybe they hadn't left earlier than she thought for the cruise, but she stopped in the kitchen for a drink and saw the small turkey breast in the refrigerator for heating up the next day. Why bother with more?

She went right when she reached the top of the stairs, away from their master suite to the room furthest away. She flipped on the light in her room and it was exactly as she left it. She curled on her bed not bothering to get changed into night clothing and fell asleep.

It was ten by the time she woke up, and she jumped out of bed, scrambling to orientate herself. This was late for her. The drive must have taken more out of her than she thought, and despite all the coffee she drank between New York and Orlando, she'd crashed hard. She took a quick shower and twisted her wet hair into her standard bun, then went downstairs. Her uncle sat at the breakfast table, and her aunt was in the kitchen.

"Morning," she said, attempting a smile on her face. She wasn't sure if it was convincing, but it was the best she could. "What are you cooking? It smells good."

"Just put some bread in the oven," her aunt said. "How was the drive? When did you get back?"

"Around midnight last night. The house was dark so I assumed you were in bed and didn't want to wake you." Jamie took an apple off the table and bit into it. "As far as the drive, there were plenty of people I swear don't know how to drive, but I managed to live." She shrugged. Her uncle made a derisive sound and snapped his newspaper. Jamie chewed the apple, tamping down the knot in her gut that had been growing since she crossed the Florida state line. "Rule number one. Never turn down free food."

"And we can see you've been following that rule," her uncle mumbled.

Wait was that a joke? Jamie gave a small dry laugh.

"Only the good stuff."

"Tim, she's just come home. Let's not tease. Sit, Jamie, tell us about school. Any boys? How are classes?"

Jamie did as she said and sat down at the table with her uncle. Her aunt took off the apron and sat with them.

"Classes are fine. It's mostly general education stuff, but I love my anthropology class and the professor. I guess he's kind of turned into my mentor." She took another bite of the apple. "My two best friends are boys, Scott and Duncan, and they're roommates, but that's all I can say about *boys*." She shrugged. "That's about it." She realized she didn't want to tell them about the new job, or how she and Scott liked the same books, or how Amy was crazy. All that was too significant, too personal.

"Who is this professor you mentioned," her uncle asked, scowling.

"Doctor Bond," she said, realizing too late she'd given away too much.

"Jamie, I don't like the sound of this," her aunt said with a shake of her head. "I've heard far too many terrible stories about older men in positions of authority taking advantage of young girls."

"Ewww, Aunt Jane." Jamie shuddered. "That's just gross!"

"And these two boys are roommates?" There it was; there was her out.

"Yes," she nodded. "Makes it easy to hang out. I just go to their dorm and do homework."

"It sounds like you have gotten into a routine. That's good," Aunt Jane said.

"I hardly call going to a boys' dorm good." Uncle Tom scowled his disapproved.

"Come on, Uncle Tim, you can't tell me you never had girls in your dorm. Probably even Aunt Jane." Jamie rolled her eyes taking another bit of the apple to keep her mouth occupied.

"Which is precisely why I know these boys have other things on their mind than your English notes."

Jamie gasped and shot out of her chair. "Geez, is that what you think of me? I'm off at college being seduced by older teachers and roommates? I'm there for an education."

The silence hung like a heavy fog. She rounded the table and headed for the kitchen. "Coffee? I've developed a dependency on the stuff." She bit her lip, focusing on the pinch to distract her, and tossed her apple in the trash as she passed.

"You'd better be focusing on your education. Not many students have hefty trust funds to send them to school," her uncle spoke.

Aunt Jane gasped. "Tim!"

"Actually, Uncle Tim, you're wrong. A *lot* of students at Clarkmore attend on trust funds, but given the alternative, I'd gladly put myself into debt up to my eyeballs *not* to have a trust fund and *have* parents." Anger collided with the hurt she'd been smothering for months. "Is that what you think of me? You know I worked hard to get into Clarkmore, and most of my tuition is paid for by scholarships."

"And the rest is paid for by a check issued by your financial advisor," he said with poison in his tone. "He called, by the way, asking how he could reach you. I felt pretty stupid not knowing you'd hired one."

"I'm eighteen, Uncle Tim. I can do with it what I want. And yeah, a whole fifteen hundred dollars. Out of the total of over fifteen thousand for tuition. I think I did well." She whipped around and looked at them. "I work on the school newspaper, I'm getting good grades, and I have good friends. All without you." She closed her eyes and rubbed her temples. "I've planned, I've been careful, I've learned how to take care of myself from now on, because I knew once I turned eighteen I was on my own. When are you leaving for your cruise, by the way?" she tossed out, not even attempting to hide her sarcasm.

"What does that have to do with what you're doing at school?" Tim stood up from the chair.

"Because most students don't have to find another place to stay for Christmas because their 'family' is going on a six-month cruise!" she shouted. "Thanks for the letter of support by the way. Really read as heartfelt."

"Why did you even come back for Thanksgiving?"

"Tim, please stop..."

"Because I figured I needed to see you once before you left. As crazy as this sounds, maybe I didn't want to wait until summer break to see you again." She rolled her eyes, angry at the burn of tears. "Would you have rather I hadn't come back?"

"Tim, Jamie, stop this now," Jane chimed in. "Both of you need to calm down."

"Just when did you decide I was such a drain?" Jamie asked, not realizing it was the one question she ever had. "You know, when Mom and Dad were alive I used to look so forward to when you came to visit. You were my only aunt and uncle, but you were still my *favorite* aunt and uncle. I thought coming to live with you would make it okay. I thought—" She stuttered on the last sentence and had to stop.

Aunt Jane stood slowly and stepped toward her, holding out a hand. "Oh, Jamie. It's not like that at all. We just—"

"You just didn't want me."

"We never said we didn't want you."

"Not *to* me!" she shouted. "You just waited until you thought I was out of earshot and talked about all the things you *couldn't* do because of me. Well, congratulations. You survived the last eight years and I'm not your responsibility anymore."

"Jamie," Jane spoke, her voice soft and apologetic.

"No, I don't want to hear it. You can't apologize for eight years of that with one word. There's no fixing it." She looked at the floor and sniffed. "I'm going to go back to school."

"You don't need to do that, Jamie," Aunt Jane said, taking a step toward her.

"Yeah, I think I do."

"When are you going to leave?"

"Now." Jamie walked past them and up the stairs. She heard nothing as she grabbed her suitcase, barely unpacked because all she'd taken out was what she needed to shower, and went down the steps. She stood in the entryway of the breakfast nook where they still sat. Her aunt looked at her with red eyes, but Jamie ignored them.

"Doctor Bond is my mentor and my friend because he's a father without a daughter and he cares about me. He lost a daughter, and I lost my parents. Seems appropriate we can be friends. Duncan can be a jerk, but Scott is my best friend. They're the boys you're so worried about, Uncle Tim." They stared at her, saying nothing, although she expected them to say something. Anything. "I'll see you over summer vacation. When I come to get my things. I think it's time I find someplace else to live. I don't want to be a burden anymore."

She felt a finality as she got in her truck, a truck she'd bought herself. She felt no sense of farewell as she drove away. She wasn't leaving home. Home had been about fifteen miles east, with a pool in the backyard and a boxer named Rocky.

Jamie drove a few hours before her stomach dug at her to eat. The apple had given up on her. She pulled off the highway and into a McDonalds. Ordering her food she sat down at a table and pulled out her phone.

I'm going back to school. I tried. I really did.

There was a long pause before she got a response from Doctor Bond.

Where are you now?

South Carolina

Are you okay?

I feel kind of hollow. I don't feel like I left anything behind.

Do you need to talk?

I'm okay.

Drive safe. We'll talk when you get back. Let
me know when you get here. I'll meet you for
coffee.

Responding with a 'K', Jamie ate her food and refilled her large drink with a mix of Dr. Pepper and Coke, a charge of caffeine to get her some distance, and drove further away from her past.

IT WAS MID-MORNING THE NEXT DAY BY THE TIME SHE MADE IT BACK TO school. She ended up pulling off into a rest area and slept in her truck for a few hours when she was too tired to drive safely. Amy was gone and wouldn't be back until Sunday. She went home a day before vacation began, missing a day of classes, so for once Jamie had the dorm room to herself. No craziness, no walking on eggshells. Jamie curled onto her bed, pulling the blanket over her head, and fell asleep. There were so many places she would rather be at the moment. Neither Florida nor her dorm was on that list, and she realized as she slipped into sleep she had become accustomed to being with friends and missed them.

She missed Scott.

One vibration of her phone she could sleep through, but the constant vibration pulled her out of sleep. Jamie fumbled in her blankets, half asleep, to her phone somewhere on her bed. Finally, she found it and saw Doctor Bond's face on the screen, a picture she's snapped one day much to his faked annoyance.

"Hello," she mumbled, still half asleep. She was unsure what day it was or what time.

"What are you doing right now?" Doctor Bond asked.

"Sleeping."

'Do you get my many text messages?"

"I've been asleep," she responded. "What time is it?" She groaned a weird laugh. "Heck, what day is it?"

"Eleven in the morning the day before Thanksgiving." She knew what he was doing by the tone of voice. He was pinching the bridge of his nose and rolling his eyes. Jamie smiled. "It sounds like you could use that coffee."

"Let me take a shower. How does an hour sound?" she responded, sitting up and rubbing her eyes with her free hand.

"Let's just call it lunch. When was the last time you ate?"

Jamie had to pause before she answered that one. "McDonald's on the way home. Last I texted you."

She heard his sigh. "Meet me at that pizza place you like. I'll buy lunch. And, I'll bring you some turkey."

"You don't have to do that, Doctor Bond."

"Beth already cooked it, and we certainly aren't going to eat it all. I will see you in an hour."

Jamie hung up the phone and pulled her hair out of the bun

JAMIE SAT AT A TABLE IN THE CORNER OF MARIO'S, WAITING FOR Doctor Bond, holding a large Dunkin' Donuts coffee in her hand keeping them warm as she clutched the cup. Winter had finally arrived in New York, and it had arrived with a vengeance.

Doctor Bond came through the door with a gust of wind and snow. He crossed the pizzeria with a fabric grocery bag hanging off his arm, pulling off his gloves. He looked tired. Out of it. Was he short on breath, or was that because of the wind? Jamie smiled when she saw him, already feeling some of the heavy tension ease. It was good to see a smiling face. He placed the bag on the floor by her feet. He stood there and Jamie could tell he was out of it.

"Are you alright, Doctor Bond? You seem out of breath."

"Wind takes it away from me from time to time. Here you go." He pointed to the bag he'd set on the floor.

Jamie smiled and looked up at him. "Thank you"

"Absolutely. Enjoy the rhubarb pie. It's my favorite." Doctor Bond sat down and adjusted his coat. "What happened?"

"I didn't start it, just so you know. Aunt Jane asked about school, that kind of thing. But every time I answered a question, Uncle Tim twisted what I said into something..." She winced and shook her head. "Vulgar and perverted. I couldn't even believe..." She shook her head again and shrugged. "Then, he's throwing in my face I should be paying more attention to school because not all college students get their tuition paid by a nice trust fund." The words caught in her throat. They still hurt.

He didn't say anything. He just reached across the table and wrapped his hand over hers. Jamie pressed her lips together and looked away. She swallowed and squeezed his hand before she got the flood of emotions under control.

"I told them I'm moving out next summer," she told him, taking a deep breath. "I don't have much in the house, but I have a lot in storage. When the house was sold, the will said the profit of the house would go to my aunt and uncle to cover the expenses of caring for me, but the rest of their estate went into a trust. I remember going through the house with my aunt. She helped me choose things to keep: photos and albums, my mother's jewelry and keepsakes, and my father's music collection. He liked jazz," she said with a smile and a chuckle. "He played saxophone. I have it. I never learned to play, though."

"It's good you have those things."

She nodded. "It wasn't always like this with my aunt and uncle. I mean, maybe it was but I don't remember it. Maybe I was too dazed, maybe I was too naïve, but I remember them taking care of me and talking to me and seeming to care." Sadness rolled in her chest again. "I don't know what I did—"

"Stop," he said, snatching her hand again across the table. "Don't even say it, Jamie. You did nothing. You were a child who needed to be loved. I won't even begin to hypothesize what went on in their heads, but it doesn't matter. You did nothing wrong."

She just nodded and sniffed.

"You have a plan, and you have a future. You know what you want, and I have so much faith in you that you will have it all. You will be happy, despite it all."

Jamie looked at him and swallowed the lump in her throat. It felt so good to have someone say they had faith in her. "Thank you."

He smiled and winked and took back his hand, leaning back in his chair. "Now, how are your studies?"

Jamie chuckled and canted her head. "How are my *studies*," she teased. "Sometimes it's so obvious you didn't grow up here. You know, besides the accent."

"I don't have an accent," he said automatically, their joke.

"Uh-huh. I have A's in everything. I'm not concerned with that." She waved it off and crossed her arms in front of her chest.

"Good. Keep focused, that's what's important. And don't forget the people who care about you."

"Yeah, I know," she muttered. She looked back up at him and he smiled.

Jamie fell on her bed and pulled one of the blankets she kept at the foot up and over her head. She had been driving for so long. Before she let herself drift off into a long, glorious sleep she pulled out her phone.

> Scott, I came back to New York. Home wasn't what I was expecting it to be. Or… maybe it was.

Pressing send, she dropped her phone on the bed beside her and closed her eyes. The Star Wars theme song pulled her out of a dreamless sleep. Scrambling for her phone, it took her a moment to find it and another to get her eyes to focus on the caller ID screen. Scott.

"Hi," she mumbled, too groggy for more. Could she not just take a nap?

"What are you doing back at school?" he asked

"I told you in the text message," she answered, burying her face head-first into the pillow. "It was awful," she muttered.

"Thanksgiving is tomorrow."

"I know."

"What are you going to do?"

Jamie paused and rolled to face the wall. She hadn't thought about it. The cafeteria was closed and the campus was practically empty.

"Subway."

She heard the scoff come from Scott over the phone. "I don't think so. Hang on." His voice was slightly softer when he spoke again like he didn't have the phone right to his mouth. "Mom. Jamie is back at school. She doesn't have a place to be for Thanksgiving." There was a pause and some muffled talking. Jamie figured he covered the speaker. She would have argued, would have fought back, but she was still half asleep and didn't care at the moment. Then more shuffling. "Come here, Jamie."

"What?"

"Mom said she wants you to come over for the holiday. Get in your truck and drive to my house," Scott said. "I'll text you my address."

"Scott, I can't—"

"Yes. You can." He paused. "Jamie, I want you here."

She groaned. "Can I sleep for a little bit?" she asked. "I'm half asleep now."

"Yes, sleep first and then come. Just call or text before you leave so Mom will know when to officially worry." He chuckled. "You're going to have Thanksgiving Scotch style."

Jamie had the directions plugged into her truck GPS, and she drove another nearly six hours to Scott's house. In all truth, she was sick of driving and had paid far too much in gas over the past few days. She ended up sleeping way into the night, longer than she had planned, and woke early the next morning. It was a much later start than she wanted, and she would be there sometime late morning *on* Thanksgiving day, but she needed the sleep before she drove that far. It would have been dangerous for her to drive when she was as exhausted mentally and physically as she was. It had been a hard, dreamless sleep; a sign to her that she needed the sleep more than she thought. Jamie was grateful she decided to wait before driving, but just to be safe during the entire drive she had her music blasting and the windows rolled down. A loud noise and a gust of fresh air.

She felt better once she pulled off the freeway, knowing she neared his house. The cluster of businesses, stores, and apartment buildings eventually faded into rural communities and neighborhoods. One street would be older homes, dating back probably a hundred years or more, then she'd drive further into the neighborhood and the houses changed to newer styles and the streets were more exact, straight rather than winding and curvy. Eventually, her GPS informed her "Your destination is on the right," and she found Scott's home.

The neighborhood was newer, the houses nice sized but not crazy big like some she had driven past. In Florida, where she lived, most of the homes were in planned developments with carefully sized yards and protruding garages that greeted anyone pulling into the driveway. You couldn't see into the next neighbor's house, but you could hear a good fight. In this neighborhood, the spacing was nicer; an easy stroll to the neighbor. His house was set in the curve of a cul-de-sac with a driveway long enough to park three cars bumper to bumper. It was simple, and as corny as it sounded, welcoming: dark beige with white shutters, two stories, with a closed-in porch across the front. Just by the way the houses sat, she'd put money on a nice-sized backyard. A basketball hoop hung on the front of the two-stall garage at the top of the driveway.

It was about eleven before she pulled into his driveway. She sat there for a minute after she turned off the truck, looking at the house. A giddy nervousness twisted in her stomach. What had she been thinking? Really? Barging in on Scott and his family on *Thanksgiving*? For one irrational minute, she considered turning the truck back on, backing out of the driveway, and calling him from somewhere on the Cross Bronx Expressway. With a huff, she climbed out of the truck, set the alarm, and walked to the door.

She had just gathered the nerve to raise her hand and knock on the doorframe when the door opened.

"Jamie," Scott said way too enthusiastically and pulled her into a hug. A hug she gladly returned. She probably hung on a little longer than she needed to because in just a couple of days she'd missed his hugs. And, she needed one.

"Wow, were you waiting by the door?" She laughed.

"No, I was walking by and saw you sitting in the truck. Come inside, we'll get your stuff in a few minutes. My Dad and Lois are supposed to be here any minute now, and after we all catch up we'll eat."

"Is my truck in the way?"

"No, you're good. There's plenty of room."

Jamie smiled "Okay. I'm sorry it took so long for me to get here. I just really needed to sleep."

"Don't worry about it. You got here before the food, so that's all that matters," Scott said, then cupped his hand around his mouth. "Mom, Jamie is here!" He took her hand and pulled her into the house. "Come inside before the house gets cold."

Jamie shuffled in, cleaning the snow off her sneakers before she stepped inside, and shut the door behind her. She only had a minute to take a look around. The foyer opened to the left and right into rooms and a staircase sitting in front of her led to the second level. A row of coats and boots hung along one wall, and with a quick look, she saw the room to her left was a large living room. To the right was a smaller sitting room with a dining room beyond. The floors were wood and the house smelled like roasted turkey. Her stomach grumbled. Scott helped her take her coat off and hung it on one of the hooks by the door.

"Hello, Jamie." Jamie turned to the voice and saw Scott's mom coming into the foyer. At least she assumed it was his mom based on the pictures in his dorm. She was a little shorter than Jamie, with blond hair and dark eyes, though not as dark as Scott's. Smile lines bracketed her eyes. "I'm Nora, Scott's mother."

Jamie took the hand extended out to her.

"Hi. Thank you so much for inviting me. It means a lot."

"Oh, I couldn't have you at school by yourself for the holiday; not when you and Scott are such good friends. And Thanksgiving is a time to open your house to people. Please come on in. Can I get you some tea? It's cold outside."

"Some tea would be amazing."

Jamie smiled. This was so new to her. The house seemed so... friendly. And his father and Lois were coming too. Why could her family not be like this?

The doorbell went off. Jamie reached behind her and opened the door. She was the closest one to it.

"Hey, you're a new face," Scott's dad said, looking surprised.

"Oh, sorry. I'm Jamie," she answered, taking a step back. Before she could understand, she was pulled into another hug. Now, she could see where Scott got his hugging from. It was nice.

"So you're Jamie. I have heard so much about you. I'm Richard, Scott's father, and this is Lois, my wife." Scott's father was considerably taller than Jamie, by a head and a half at least, with light brown hair and blue eyes. Scott was a balanced mix between them, just with hair and eyes a shade darker than both. Lois, his stepmother, was a petite woman with long, straight, black hair and angled eyes.

"Good things, I hope," Jamie joked, glancing at Scott.

"Only the best." He shut the door and walked into the room.

"Hello, Richard," Nora said with a smile. "Oh, Lois, you brought your amazing date nut bread, thank you." She took the wrapped package from Lois and turned to the staircase. "Amber! Come down here," Nora yelled up the stairs.

"Coming!" A young girl ran down the stairs, a younger version of Nora. "Hey, Dad. Lois. New girl."

"I'm Jamie," she said, giving an awkward wave.

"Cool."

"Amber, Jamie is going to be staying here for a few days. Can she sleep in your room with you?" their mom asked.

Jamie held her breath. She was waiting for the blow-up. The blow-off. Whatever.

"Yeah, sure, that's fine."

Jamie felt bad because she was in such shock, and just knew it was all over her face. She never had siblings, but she always heard they were supposed to fight and give each other a hard time, so to see something like that happen so easily – to have your brother's friend show up without any real notice and then have her sleep in your room with you – go over so well went against everything Jamie thought would happen.

Everyone migrated into the living room to the left of the foyer, and Jamie just followed the crowd. Scott motioned for her to sit on a loveseat, and when she did, he sat beside her. Jamie was hit with question after question, some she didn't want to answer.

"So why are you not with family today?" Lois asked

She slid a glance at Scott before she answered, "My family is in Florida."

She stumbled over the word "family." It wasn't a total lie. She just left out the part about her "family" being just as happy she wasn't there as she had been happy to leave. Scott's arm rested across the back of the loveseat and his fingers gently squeezed the back of her neck, letting her know it was okay. So maybe he hadn't told them everything, or maybe not told *everyone* everything. She was okay with that because she wouldn't be the pathetic orphan girl that way. The answer seemed to be enough for everyone to move on. They talked for a good hour and a half, Jamie was very grateful when Nora said the food was ready. The quick pull of turkey from the food Doctor Bond had given her wasn't going to hold her off much longer.

The feast was huge! Not only was there turkey and all the fixings she kind of expected for the holiday – stuffing, bread, potatoes, turnips, cranberry sauce – but there was also a ton of Chinese food. She remembered Scott said they always had Chinese food the night before the holiday. Jamie never celebrated Thanksgiving with her aunt and uncle. Their dinner on Thanksgiving wasn't a traditional Thanksgiving meal, nothing fancy. And they all got a few days off work or school. Her uncle was American, yes, but his family had emigrated from South Korea just before he had been born. Just like his excuse for not celebrating Christmas, Uncle Tim claimed his family hadn't adopted the American holiday. Jamie didn't buy that story either. His given name was Timothy, and for a family he claimed wanted to hang on to their heritage, it always struck her odd they would name him Timothy if they didn't want him to embrace his country of birth.

But hey, what was one more excuse?

There was more talking going around the table. As much as Jamie did talk along with them, she was more focused on the amazing meal. Scott sat next to her and ate just as much as she did.

"Enjoying the food?" he asked just after Jamie had taken a large bite of her roll. She simply nodded in response and kept eating.

Dessert was just as large and diverse as the meal itself with three different kinds of pies – apple, pumpkin, and chocolate cream – fudge, cookies, along with something his mom called a trifle. The meal seemed like it could feed two dozen people, or more, and yet here they were all six of them stuffing their faces and talking... having fun.

This was the most fun she had had at someone's house, her own included, in a very long time. And, the food coma that took over just a few hours later was well deserved.

AN AIR MATTRESS WAS SET UP FOR HER IN AMBER'S ROOM ON THE FLOOR. It was more than she could ask for. Scott brought her blankets and a huge stack of pillows, and when he got strange looks from his mother and sister about the quantity, Scott explained she slept with four in the dorm room. His mother's look was only slightly stranger when he told her about the pillows, but she went on a pillow hunt anyway.

"Can I ask you a question?" Amber asked later that night as they both lay on the beds, letting the food digest from the day's meal.

A meal Jamie wasn't ever going to forget.

"Go ahead," she responded, looking up at the ceiling.

Moving was a challenge at the moment, but a challenge Jamie was okay with having. Eating all that food, the laughter, the talking, made her remember holidays and meals when she was much younger. She thought it should hurt, or something, but it didn't. It felt good to remember and to connect those old memories to the memories she made today.

"Scott said you *did* go back to Florida, but you came back. What happened?"

So Scott *did* talk about why she was in the dorm room the day before Thanksgiving.

Jamie rolled her head on the pillow to look at Scott's sister. Amber was stretched out on her bed on her side, her head held up on the heel of her hand. She was a nice kid, really sweet. Jamie also realized she'd never heard Scott talk bad about his sister, like how she was a pain, or getting in trouble. They kidded with each other, but she could tell it was all just fun.

"My parents died when I was young, and I live with my aunt and uncle, but we don't get along," she explained. "We used to. When my parents were alive, we got along great, but when my parents died my aunt and uncle became my guardians. We haven't seen eye-to-eye since."

"So you came back because you started fighting?"

Jamie nodded. "It was strange. It was a fight, but not like a normal fight. I told them they weren't fooling anyone, I knew how they felt about me, and I wasn't going to live like that anymore, and they didn't take to it very well."

"That kinda sucks. But...I'm glad you came. All we've heard since Scott came home is stories about you."

Amber rolled over, and Jamie gave a small laugh. Not too hard of one since that would involve putting pressure on her stomach. "At least they were good stories," she whispered rolling over and drifting off to sleep.

Jamie woke up on her own after probably the best sleep she'd had in a long time. Amber's bed was empty, and the sun shone bright through the window. Jamie reached over to her side and grabbed her phone.

"Three in the afternoon? Jeez!"

She quickly moved from her bed and grabbed her clothing, dashing into the bathroom to grab the quickest shower in the history of man and make herself look somewhat decent. Twisting her damp hair in a messy bun, she went downstairs. The sound of three voices carried from the living room where they had all sat the day before, and just below the sound of talking was music. Christmas music. Jamie trod carefully, wondering if she should try to slip past the room to the kitchen and leave them to whatever they were doing. She'd already imposed so much.

"Oh, good, you're awake," Nora said as Jamie tried to pass the archway.

Scott's mother knelt on the floor beside a large plastic bin, a pile of red beaded garland beside her. The smell of evergreen drifted into the hall. Amber sat cross-legged on the couch with a tree skirt spread in her lap, and Scott stood beside an eight-foot Christmas tree, a *real* tree, cutting away the branch bindings. He looked at her across the room, winked, and smiled.

"We were just about to start decorating the Christmas tree. Would you like to help?" his mother asked, removing a bundle of lights from the bin.

Jamie blinked, surprised once again. Christmas had been celebrated with her aunt and uncle, yes, but it was never a big thing. They had a small store-bought tree; so small it could sit on the table as a centerpiece and came out of the box pre-decorated. They didn't do anything more than one gift to each other. There were no stockings like the ones already laid out on the mantle for hanging. There had been no lighted garland on the staircase or wreath on the door. And *no* Christmas music.

"I...sure," she finally managed to say and walked across the room to stand next to Scott while he fluffed the branches. The heady scent of pine filled her senses and made her nose tingle and her eyes water. At least she was convinced it was the pine. "Sorry, I slept half the day away. I guess driving as much as I did took a lot out of me. More than I realized."

"We figured as much. That's why we didn't wake you up. Are you hungry? There's eggnog in the kitchen, and I can make you something to eat."

"I'm okay," she answered softly, her voice caught somewhere in her throat. "I can eat when the tree is done."

He smiled and went to the spot where his mother had laid out the lights. "Lights go first. You can help by unwinding them as I wrap them. Okay?"

Jamie nodded. "Okay."

It was a new world to Jamie or an old one long since passed and nearly forgotten. Setting up the Christmas tree, large dinners of leftovers from Thanksgiving, music, and decorations. Doing things together. All things she hadn't had for eight years. Things she thought died a long time ago. She loved it.

Jamie sat at the table in her childhood house, doing homework — no — getting frustrated with biology in general. Who would do this stuff willingly? None of it made sense to her nine-year-old mind. Biology? Animals? Cells? What is this madness?

Her parents walked into the room and her mother leaned over her shoulder to look at her paper. "You're getting the right answers," her mother assured her, smoothing her hand over Jamie's hair. Her mother was good at this stuff. She liked science, but it was still confusing to Jamie.

"Mom, when is Christmas?" she asked, looking up at her mother as she put down her pencil. The tree was in the living room, all set up and decorated, so it had to be soon.

"Next week. You have to wait seven more days for Santa to come," her father chimed in, moving on into the kitchen.

"Do I still have to go to school?"

Both her parents laughed. "Yes, Jamie, you still have to go to school," her mother answered. "And, you still have to do your science homework. You have to finish that English essay, too."

Jamie pouted. "Santa doesn't have to go to school."

"He went to school already," her mother said, hugging her. "He did all his school already, and you know what? I think he even liked science."

Jamie made a face. "I don't know who would like science."

Jamie woke up slowly from the dream. It wasn't a nightmare or a bad dream, leaving her short of breath and shaking like she had become used to. It hadn't been a dream at all, but a memory she'd locked away in some part of her mind. She remembered it now, remembered the way the house had smelled of cinnamon and sugar cookies and evergreens. The way her father would play Christmas music with a jazzy twist on his saxophone. The way she ran through the house on Christmas morning shouting that Santa had come and left stacks of beautifully wrapped presents and a stocking overflowing with little goodies.

The room was dark, with a glow from the moon outside reflecting off the light layer of snow. Amber was sound asleep. Jamie stood up from the air mattress and eased her way out of the room, not wanting to wake the girl and explain why she was up in the middle of the night. She needed to think. She felt out of sorts, not sure she should be wandering around Scott's house in the middle of the night. Jamie just needed to settle somewhere and clear her head, let herself get sleepy again so she could go back to bed. As she walked around the house, she decided rather quickly that sitting in front of a lit-up Christmas tree would be the perfect spot.

She turned on the lights to the Christmas tree, the twinkling colors and glowing white bulbs filling the otherwise dark room with a beautiful glow, and curled up on the couch, covering herself with the blanket and sitting on the back of the cushions. The amount of lights on the tree was insane but absolutely perfect.

This home was everything she remembered and everything she wanted. Yes, it wasn't the perfect dream. It wasn't what she thought she had wanted, but it was so full of love, kindness, and happiness, and it made her miss her parents all over again.

"Jamie?" a voice she knew was Scott's whispered from the doorway.

"Yes?" she asked.

He walked around the couch and sat down at her feet. He wore red plaid flannel pajama pants and a white tee shirt, his hair rumpled and sticking up a little. She smiled but decided not to tease. He leaned his head on the back of the couch and stared at her, smiling. "Wow, your hair really is long."

Jamie smiled. "Not many people have seen it down, so you should feel very special. You might be the first since..." She swallowed, but smiled, and looked at him. "Since my mom. I always tuck it up like she did." She chuckled, feeling strangely nervous. "I already told you all that. I'm sorry."

"It's okay." He draped his arm across the back of the couch and touched her hair with his fingertips. "It shines with the lights."

Jamie felt heat rise in her cheeks and looked away from him.

"What are you doing up?" he asked.

"I had a dream, and I needed to think about it."

"A bad dream?"

Jamie shook her head. "More like a lost memory." She looked at the tree again. "We did a good job. It's beautiful." She smiled.

"You're beautiful."

Jamie looked at him and smiled, not minding the blush so much anymore. "Well, you're kinda perfect."

Scott slid his hand from the back of the couch and touched her shoulder. Jamie shifted and scooted across the couch to curl against him. *Everything* was perfect.

Scott had always been there for her, in ways she hadn't realized until now. She could text him anytime, about anything, and he always answered. He knew her better than anyone ever had, ever.

With a bloom of warmth in her chest she realized Scott made her happy.

Wasn't that what he said? *You can be happy without being perfect.*

Guess it depended on your definition of perfect.

They sat in silence for a long time, just watching the lights on the tree. Jamie drew in a deep pine and cinnamon-scented breath, the heavy feeling of impending sleep drifting over her.

She liked being able to sit here, quiet, and enjoy.

"Are you going to stay through Sunday and go to school at the same time I am?" Scott asked, breaking the silence. "I'd planned on heading back Sunday afternoon."

"If that's alright," Jamie answered, turning enough to look at him.

"It's more than alright," he answered with a smile. "We go to church on Sunday. We'll ask you to come."

"I'll come." She smiled. "In fact, I'm glad you invited me." She snaked her arm out from under the blanket and placed her hand on his. "Thank you for being amazing, Scott."

"Ha! I'm not amazing," he said with a shake of his head. He turned his hand over to hold hers.

"Yeah. You're better than amazing."

Chapter Eleven

Jamie had the most amazing four days of her life, or at least since she was a little. They had to rank right up there with trips to Fantasyland at the Magic Kingdom when she was little and still believed in fairytales and Prince Charming. After Friday night, sitting in the living room with Scott to watch the Christmas lights, she spent part of Saturday with Nora and Amber shopping. Nora said it was time she had a "Girls' Day," because it sounded like she hadn't had one in a while.

By the end of the trip, Jamie's fingernails had been buffed and shined, her toenails were painted alternating purple and green, and her traditional bun had been swapped for an intricate braid she hated to finally take out before she went to bed.

The other part of the day she spent with Scott and just Scott. He took her into the city, and they walked through Times Square to see the holiday lights. Rockefeller Square was decorated except for the tree. She was a week early for decorating. It didn't matter. Everything was beautiful. It took her breath away. They found a theater running classic Christmas movies back to back, and they sat through *White Christmas* before heading home.

Sunday she attended church with Scott and his family. She had braced herself for strange looks like people would wonder who she was and why she was there, but instead, she saw more people just like Scott and his family. Everyone smiled, everyone greeted her and welcomed her, and no one asked or cared why she was there. When she and Scott finally left for school, him in his car and her in her truck, she felt lighter than she could ever remember.

Monday afternoon, Jamie sat next to Scott in Anthropology, her back against the wall and her foot propped up on Scott's legs. At the beginning of the class everyone sat quiet, waiting for Doctor Bond's usual dramatic arrival, but by quarter past conversation milled through the room.

"I wonder where Doctor Bond is?" she asked, looking at the clock.

Yes, he had a habit of being late, but late for him was five minutes. This was nearly fifteen minutes

"Send him a text," Scott said, nodding his head to the phone she had sitting on the table.

Jamie picked it up. "Yeah." A heavy lump sat in her stomach like something was wrong, but she shook it off. She just saw him a few days before. What could have happened since then?

> Hey, Where are you? We do have class today, remember? ha-ha

Another five minutes passed before the classroom door opened. Jamie sat up, ready to give Doctor Bond a teasing look, but stopped. Doctor Melody June, the president of the school, walked down the aisle to the front of the room. Jamie was shocked. She had seen photos of the iconic woman around campus and heard she gave talks now and then, but she had never seen her in person. Jamie's heart started pounding so hard it hurt. She sank back into her chair and reached blindly for Scott. His hand caught hers.

"I see her," he said.

Doctor June reached the front of the classroom and cleared her voice, bringing the near-silent room to a painful still. Jamie held her breath, her lungs aching. She squeezed Scott's hand in desperation.

"Students, I'm very sorry to be the bearer of bad news."

Jamie choked on a gasp. "Oh, God..."

"Doctor Bond collapsed on Saturday. I don't know specifics, nor could I share them if I did."

"Scott..." Jamie choked.

He came out of his chair and knelt beside her, wrapping his arm around her. Jamie started to shake. She couldn't stop.

"He is currently in Intensive Care, but we have heard nothing further about his condition."

"He's alive?" Jamie burst out, her voice echoing in the smothering room.

Doctor June looked to the back of the room and made eye contact with Jamie. "Yes," she said, but her voice sounded false, unsure. "He is getting the best possible care."

The "but.." hung in the air unsaid. She just saw him a few days ago. He had been fine. He promised he wouldn't leave her. He promised he wouldn't–

"I know," Scott said, leaning his forehead against the side of her hair. She realized she'd been saying everything aloud.

"All of your grades are being placed on academic hold and whatever your current grade is, that will be the standing grade for the semester. There will be no class for the rest of the term, and no final exam. We are close enough to the end of the term, we felt the decision was appropriate."

The rest of Doctor June's words faded out.

Jamie just texted him, and teased him for being late. Asking where he was.

She *just* texted him.

She just *saw* him.

Doctor June stopped talking and everyone stood, filing out of the room. Their voices were gibberish. Nothing made sense. Tears burned in her eyes, but she couldn't blink.

She trusted him.

She told him everything.

He promised her he would be here to see her children.

"Jamie." Scott's voice edged through the vicious pounding in her head. "Come on. Let's go away from everyone. Come on."

He took her hand and she let him draw her out of the chair and drape his coat over her shoulders. She felt his arm slide around her back, knew he had taken her bag, knew he led her across campus to his dorm, but she couldn't think past that. Her eyes burned. Her lungs burned. Her chest hurt. And she couldn't stop shaking. They reached his room and she stood in the hall shaking while he unlocked the door. The room beyond was dark, Duncan wasn't there. Scott set her bag on the floor by the door and reached for the light switch, but she stopped him.

He nodded and took his coat off her shoulders and tossed it aside, then wrapped her in his arms and held her. Jamie collapsed into him, sucking in what felt like her first breath in fifteen minutes.

"It's going to be okay, Jamie," Scott spoke gently, rubbing her back.

She shook her head against this chest.

"No, no it's not. Not if he d-dies! He's the only father I know, and he isn't even *mine*." A sob ripped from her. She tightened her grip on Scott and he held her tighter.

She cried until it hurt and then cried some more. Her legs eventually gave out, and Scott held her up until she made it to his bed. She collapsed on the floor beside it, not even able to crawl onto the soft mattress. Scott sat beside her and embraced her again, holding her tight.

It couldn't be real. This was a bad dream. She was asleep in her dorm room. This was a turkey-induced dream, hung over from Thanksgiving. She'd had this dream before that she'd lost him, but it was a dream. *A dream*! It couldn't happen. He couldn't die. She couldn't lose him.

She didn't consciously mean to say aloud all the tumbling thoughts in her head, but she had to be because Scott kept reassuring her. Doctor Bond wasn't gone. He was still alive. There was still hope.

She lost track of time, and she was sure that she had missed her next class, which meant Scott had missed a few as well, but she couldn't bring herself to let go. She rested her head in his lap and cried some more, his hand stroking her hair.

Scott kept telling her simple things. "It's going to be okay, Jamie," and "We're going to get through this. He'll get through this." But how could she believe that?

They sat there on the floor for hours. There were times she thought maybe she dozed off, or maybe she was just so lost in the fear she shut out everything, but the sun waned eventually and the room darkened. She didn't care.

Then the door opened and the light flicked on, the light searing through her head like an ice pick. Jamie covered her eyes and turned to hide her face against Scott.

"Dude, did you hear what happened? Your anthropology professor – Whoa. What is she crying about?"

"Doctor Bond," Scott answered in a softer voice than Duncan. His hand smoothed her hair, long gone free of the bun, rubbed her shoulder, and ran his palm down her arm. The contact was soothing, and she tried to focus on that rather than the conversation or reality or anything else. She didn't want to hear Duncan, didn't want to know what was being said on campus. She just wanted to hide from the light until her crying-induced headache went away and until the whole nightmare ended. She wished Duncan would just shut up and go away and leave her alone.

Then something Duncan said snapped through her self-induced cone of silence.

"Well, I'd be glad to have any girl on my lap," he said. "And you got her hair down."

"Geez, Duncan—"

Jamie flipped back over and scrambled to her feet, her head pounding. "Are you being that much of a jerk right now?" she demanded. Pain shot from temple to temple and she was dizzy, but she still took a step toward him, and Duncan took a step back. Scott stood beside her, his hand on her arm; to hold her up or hold her back, she wasn't sure.

"I – uh – I—"

"You can't even defend yourself! How much of an idiot do you have to be to make a comment like that?" She was yelling, and people were stopping in the hall outside the room, turning and looking, but she didn't care.

"I was just saying..." He trailed off his eyes darting back and forth between her and something else. She turned to where his gaze was shifting. Scott?

"Hey, I was going to punch him," he said, holding up his hands. "But, you're making a better point. I don't know if I should stop you, or not."

Jamie turned on Duncan again.

"Did you thing he was going to help you right now?" He didn't answer. "While I'm crying you want to comment on Scott being a *friend*, you want to comment about my *hair*? Are you happy now? Wow, look it's my hair!" She flipped her hand under the loose mass, sending it flying wild in the air and around her face. "Whoa, a girl with hair! I can't get my head wrapped around this." She shook her head, then tilted it to the side and stared at Duncan. "How did I ever like you? Man, I was the stupid one."

"So, you do like me?"

Jamie glared at him, dumbfounded.

"*That's* what you comment on?"

Scott stepped around her to stand between her and Duncan. "I think you need to step off, Duncan," he said in a low, tense voice. "Don't come back for a while."

"It's my room—" he started to argue.

"Please. If you care at all, go away," Jamie pleaded, her eyes closed.

It took a moment, but he turned and walked out of the room, shutting the door behind him.

"I used to like him because I thought he had everything I thought I wanted," she said, turning to face Scott again. "I was a fool."

Scott touched her face, brushing her tussled hair back from her cheek.

"Was I a little too harsh?"

"No. He needed to be put in his place." Scott nodded. "I think you did a fine job of that."

Jamie nodded and leaned into him again.

Chapter Twelve

The next few days were a haze for Jamie. She went to class, did her work, even wrote her articles, but if anyone asked what she had just done she couldn't tell them. If it weren't for Scott checking on her, leading her to the dining hall, and texting her to go to bed she probably would have forgotten to do any of it and would still be sitting at her desk staring at the cinderblock wall.

But he had, and she wasn't a zombie, and she did what she had to do. She focused on one thing at a time and listened for any news filtered out to the students. It was minimal, and not very helpful, but she accepted it and hung on to the fact he still lived.

Thursday afternoon she was walking back to her dorm, holding her books to her chest, watching the ground as she walked and colliding with someone. Her books fell from her hands into the snow.

"I'm so sorry," she mumbled, dropping to her knees to pick up her books.

"You know that if it was anyone else I would have been angry." Jamie looked up at the sound of Duncan's voice.

"Well, at least I have that going for me," she said with a small laugh.

Duncan picked up the book nearest him and gripped her elbow

to help her stand. "Look, I wanted to apologize for what I said the other day. I should have kept my mouth shut. I wasn't thinking."

Jamie took a minute to look into his eyes, and for the first time, she thought she saw sincerity in them. She nodded. "It's fine. I forgive you. I wasn't in the best of places myself."

Duncan shoved his hands into his pockets, looking down and away before back to her. He squinted against the sun. "I know you and Scott have this thing going now, and honestly I think it's great. But do you think that we can still be friends?" he asked.

Jamie gave a small smile. It was all she could muster. She felt bad but she knew that in time she would be better. "Yeah, we can still be friends. I didn't mean to snap at you. It was just so soon..."

"Are you going to go to the service the school is having? Someone said it's like a prayer group. For a school that's not, you know, faith-based or whatever they call it, it's kinda cool they're doing this. It's just for people to come together..." He trailed off with a one-shoulder shrug.

Jamie nodded. In truth, she loved the fact the school had allowed the students to organize the show of support for Doctor Bond. "Yeah, I'm probably going to be a wreck but I'm going to go. Ha, I'm still a wreck." She gave a dry chuckle. "Amy has had about enough of me"

"I'm free to talk, you know," he said with an apologetic shrug. Shrugging was his new thing, apparently. "Open hours or not, I'd be willing to meet you somewhere and we can chat it out, get it out of your system."

"Thank you. That means a lot to me.

The next few days passed, and it seemed like she was just going through the motions. Winter break was coming up fast, but she hadn't even tried to think of where she would go. The campus was open for a short holiday like Thanksgiving, but for a long break like Christmas, she had to leave. Then she received a phone call from Nora Scotch, who asked Jamie to come to their home for the holidays. Jamie had gulped like a fish out of water for several moments before she could gather her thoughts enough to say she'd be honored to spend the holiday with them.

Then she'd cried for an hour for reasons she couldn't explain.

What a bizarre twist in her life. If she looked in one direction, she was being given the one thing she'd longed to have again: a family, people who cared about her and wanted her with them, and Scott. If she looked in the other direction, her heart was breaking at the thought she might lose Doctor Bond. He wasn't her father, she knew that, and there were so many ways he couldn't be, but she couldn't let go.

Saturday morning, Jamie's phone went off before anyone had the right to be awake on a weekend. She mumbled and fumbled around until she found it, then sat up in bed. She didn't care what time it was once she saw the name on the screen.

> Hi, Jamie. This is Beth, Andrew's wife. Let me first say he's okay, he's getting better, and he wants you to come see him. Can you?

Jamie typed so fast she was amazed autocorrect didn't have a field day with the jumbled words. Thankfully, the autocorrect gods were with her that day.

> Yes! God, yes! Today?

Her heart pounded out a rhythm. *He's okay. He's okay. He's okay.* That was all she needed to know. She didn't care it was painfully early. She didn't care about anything. She just wanted to see him.

> Today is wonderful. Visiting hours begin at four, you can come then. We will see you then.

> Thank you so much!!!!

She didn't even have to ask Scott to go with her. He had looked worried when she knocked on his door, probably looking more frantic than excited, but as soon as she told him about the text – even though she was pretty sure most of what came out of her mouth was rambling nonsense – he squeezed her hand, took her keys, and grabbed his coat.

Jamie knew she was in no shape to drive, and for the first time, let someone else behind the wheel of her beloved truck. She realized as they pulled out of the school parking lot, that she'd loved the truck when she bought it because it was hers. Something she could call her own. But now, she had more than just a truck. She had people.

It wasn't until they stepped through the doors of the hospital that her steps faltered. When the smell of antiseptic, latex, and Pine Sol hit her she thought her stomach would turn inside out. In one intake of air, she was ten years old again, being led down a hallway by the social worker who had come to bring her to see her mom.

The last time she was in a hospital was the night her mother died. The night her father was already gone.

The night everything turned upside down.

Jamie stopped.

Scott came around to stand in front of her. "Are you going to be okay?" he asked, placing his hands on her arms.

Jamie looked up at him and tried to smile. "Sooner or later."

Scott took her hand and squeezed. "You're not doing this alone, okay?" He leaned in and kissed her forehead.

She nodded and let him lead her to the elevators. Doctor Bond's wife had texted Jamie the room number, and Scott hit the correct floor button when they stepped inside. They rode up in silence, but as soon as the doors closed, Jamie leaned her head against Scott's arm. The elevator dinged and bounced to a stop. When the doors opened, she saw a nurse's station and a woman standing in the hallway, her hands held in front of her. She was pretty, with blond hair that hung past her shoulders and blue eyes. Jamie immediately thought of the picture of Doctor Bond's daughter Rachel and knew this had to be Beth.

"Are you Jamie Boyer?" the woman asked as they stepped into the hall. Jamie nodded. "I'm Beth, Andrew's wife." Her smile was genuine but strained. Jamie couldn't imagine what she had to be feeling. She wrapped Jamie in a hug. The woman felt so thin Jamie was afraid she'd break. "Thank you for coming."

"Of course," Jamie whispered as the woman let her go.

She looked at Scott. "And you must be Mr. Scotch. Jamie's constant companion."

Scott smiled, but only nodded in response.

"Is he okay?" Jamie asked, unable to wait any longer to know.

Beth smiled. "He's doing much better. I need to warn you, Jamie, he might look frightening when you see him. But, he *is* doing better."

Jamie tamped down the swell of tears in her throat. She didn't want to cry, didn't want to make his wife feel bad. "I'm so sorry," she managed to choke out. "Doctor Bond means a lot to me. I've been going crazy not knowing."

"You mean a lot to *him*, Jamie. He constantly talks about you at home; how proud he is of you for all you've been through, how much potential he sees in you." She squeezed Jamie's hand. "He never said it, because I think he was afraid it would hurt me after we lost Rachel, but I know he thinks of you as a daughter."

Jamie nodded, unable to say anything. There was some reassurance in the fact she saw him was the same as he saw her.

"I'm so grateful to know him," she finally said. "He means a lot to me." That was the third time she said he meant a lot to her, but it was true. "I mean everything I'm saying, Mrs. Bond." She gave up and let the tears run down her face, wiping them away with her thumb.

Scott wrapped his arm around her shoulder, and she leaned into him. Mrs. Bond had tears in her eyes, too.

"Since our daughter died, he has had this void nothing could fill; but in the last few months I've seen a spark in his eyes I hadn't seen in a while." She smiled at Jamie. "When he's back home, I would love you to come over to the house sometime. Have dinner with us. I want to get to know the girl he took under his wing, and still holds so close to his heart." She laughed. "We can go out sometime and make him wonder what we are talking about."

Jamie nodded. "I would love to, Mrs. Bond."

"Please call me Beth." She looked at Scott. "You're invited too, Mr. Scotch."

Jamie smiled. She liked Beth already. How could she not when the woman was planning how to pester her husband while he was still in his hospital bed?

"That would be wonderful."

JAMIE STOOD IN THE HOSPITAL ROOM DOORWAY FOR A FEW MOMENTS, steadying her heart and calming her breath, before she walked into the room. After talking to Beth she decided to go talk to him by herself. Scott was just out in the hall by the door if he was needed, but she wanted to try this alone.

The room was dim, the sun already setting outside, and only a small light by the bed illuminated the room. There were several monitors and machines near the head of the bed, each one either beeping, humming, or flashing. She tamped down the memory of her mother in a similar bed and reminded herself with a mental slap this was not then. Doctor Bond wouldn't die. He wouldn't.

"Doctor Bond?" she said softly as she walked up to the bed.

"Jamie," he said, his voice rough. Oh, it felt so good to hear him! "Come here, my girl." He smiled and raised a bandaged hand toward her.

She rushed the short distance remaining to the bed, gripping his hand in both of hers to keep from collapsing on him and hugging him. She was afraid to touch him. He was pale, his cheeks sunken showing he'd lost some weight. "I thought I lost you," she whispered, swiping at her cheek.

"That ready to get rid of me, are you?" He laughed and winked at her.

Oh, now he was joking around?

"No," she said with a chuckle, unable to return the banter just yet. She looked at the white sheets. They were so painfully white and made him look so pale.

"Jamie," he said more sternly, squeezing her hand. "Look at me." She raised her chin and met his eyes, swallowing hard. "I'm not going anywhere." His voice was calm and soothing. "I told you I intend to see *your* children."

She caught motion from the corner of her eye and saw Scott peeking in to check on her. She smiled, and he smiled back. That was enough for him to know she was okay, and he slipped from view again.

"I knew Mr. Scotch wouldn't be far behind," Doctor Bond said, sighing. "I've known since that first class, just as I knew you were someone special, Jamie, that he would be someone special for you." Jamie looked at him and he shrugged one shoulder just a small degree. "Call it intuition. Hasn't failed me yet."

Jamie cleared her throat, feeling some of the panic and worry slip away now that she could talk to him just as they always had. His voice was softer, and he wasn't throwing stress balls at her or making her coffee, but it was the same. "I went to Scott's house for Thanksgiving after you and I talked. His family is so nice. We had a huge meal, and I helped decorate the Christmas tree. Just like I belonged. And..." she proclaimed, finally letting herself enjoy the excitement. "His mother called and asked me to spend winter break with his family."

"You won't be alone."

She shook her head. "No. I don't think I'll ever be alone again."

"And he's perfect," he said.

"In so many ways," she answered.

"I know." He smiled.

FEBRUARY

JAMIE SAT ON THE FLOOR OF HER DORM ROOM, RIGHT IN FRONT OF THE heater. Winter had settled into New York with full force, and Jamie finally had to admit her Floridian skin wasn't as thick as she thought. It was snowing outside. Again. They were expecting another storm that night, one that would likely shut everyone in for Valentine's Day.

Amy sat on her bed, and they were both doing homework, the silence broken now and again by Amy cursing at something. Amy spent a lot of time cursing at her homework, and Jamie had learned to ignore her ranting. They had their dorm door open in case someone needed them. Well, more like needed something they had, but they both felt important when someone yelled their name down the hall.

And that was exactly what happened.

"Yo, Jamie!"

Scared the crap out of both of them. Jamie was halfway to her feet when Scott strolled into the room smiling, his hands behind his back.

"Who the heck screamed?" Jamie asked, sinking back down on the floor when she saw Scott. "Was that Melissa?" He nodded, grinning wider.

"Scott, what did you do to her?" Amy asked, turning around so she faced him. "That scared the crap out of me!"

"Sorry about that, Amy. I asked Melissa if she knew if Jamie was here. I guess that was her way of finding out."

Amy huffed and turned back to her desk. "Whatever."

"What are you doing here?" Jamie asked, looking at the clock. Two minutes before open hours were over.

"I needed to do this." Scott came down to his knees in front of Jamie and pulled roses and chocolates from behind his back. "I know

I'm a day early—" He glanced at her clock. "Or, an hour early, but Jamie, will you be my valentine?"

Jamie stared in shock, shaking her head. "Who-what?" she asked.

Scott was grinning like a fool. He placed the gifts on her lap, resting on top of the book she was reading, and reached into his back pocket.

"Oh god, there's more?" Amy gasped.

Scott held a finger to his lips to silence Amy and laid an envelope on the box of candies. When Jamie reached for it, he set his hand on top of it so she couldn't pick it up.

"Jamie, since that first day in the bookstore when I offered you my hand and you ignored it, I've known you were someone special. Someone I wanted in my life. I think..." He paused and grinned. "... maybe you feel that way for me?"

"Well, she sure as heck doesn't like Duncan anymore, I can tell you that much," Amy interjected, pointing for emphasis.

Jamie finally snapped her eyes over to the blond roommate. Her commentary could be funny sometimes, but right now it was the last background noise Jamie wanted to hear. Once Amy looked sufficiently contrite, Jamie turned back to Scott.

"Yes," she answered, smiling back. "I admit, it took me longer to catch a clue, but I'm so happy you're in my life." She looked down at the roses and candy. "How did you get roses?" She looked over her shoulder at the window. "How did you get anywhere? It's been snowing *all* day."

Now that her mouth was working, it wouldn't stop. Scott touched her jaw with his fingers and nudged her to turn back and look at him.

"I wasn't done yet. Jamie, will you not only be my Valentine but my girlfriend? We have already been through so much together. I want everyone to know you're my best friend, but you're so much more than that. And I want to be with you."

Her head was spinning.

"Oh, answer him, Jamie!" Amy yelled.

Jamie's eyes snapped back to her again. She had just about had enough of that.

"Amy, I *swear* I'm going to hurt you once I stand up," she promised.

She needed to stop the spinning she needed to think, but what was there to think about? Jamie looked back to Scott and nodded.

"What is that a yes to? I asked you two things."

"Yes to everything," she said with a smile so wide it hurt. "I will be your girlfriend, and I will be your Valentine." She bit her lip, a giddy feeling bubbling in her chest. Clapping burst out behind Scott. She looked around Scott and saw half of the floor standing at her door, watching. "Oh my goodness."

Scott leaned forward, and Jamie held her breath until his lips touched hers. She'd thought about kissing him, more than once, and he'd kissed her cheek or her forehead, but that was nothing compared to a real, full-lip, kiss. The bubbling in her chest spread to her head and made her dizzy.

"About dang time," Amy mumbled. "I was getting sick of watching the two of you dance around each other. The ultimate 'will they/won't they.' Ugh."

Jamie shook her head, smiling at Scott as he sat back on his heels.

"So, how did you get the flowers?" she asked again, lifting the roses to her nose to inhale the deep, heady aroma.

"Well, it wasn't easy, but you're worth it. I got them yesterday before the storm hit." He shrugged. "Again, you're worth it."

Jamie shook her head. "You have gone crazy."

"Crazy for you." Jamie rolled her eyes, and Scott laughed. "Okay, that line was bad. Can you think of a new one?"

She smiled, joking with him. "As nice as it was...no, just no." She looked at the clock again. "Oh my gosh, you have to get out of here. It's not open hours anymore; you're going to get us in trouble." She scrambled to her feet, setting aside the book and the items on top of it. Jamie grabbed his arm and dragged him toward the door. "Go! I will talk to you later." She pushed his shoulder. "Go before we all get written up. We don't do the walk of shame here."

He leaned in and kissed her one more time. "Text me?"

Jamie picked up her phone as he backed out of the room. "Already in my hands." She waved it so he could see. "Now go!"

He jogged out of the room and the army of girls from the hall left with him. She knew none of them were going to say anything; they just wanted to see what he was going to do with the flowers and candy. Jamie picked up the book and gifts and walked to her desk. She noticed the envelope he had laid on the book and wouldn't let her touch it. With a long, happy sigh Jamie opened the envelope and removed the folded paper inside.

> *Jamie,*
>
> *I have faith in you. I always will.*
>
> *I trust you. I always will.*
>
> *You are amazing, you prove that to the world every single day, and there is nothing you can do to prove me wrong. Your aunt and uncle don't know the treasure they had in you.*
>
> *But I do.*
>
> *I love you. I always will.*
>
> *Scott*

Jamie sat in her chair and cried.

"Crap." Amy huffed, twisting in her chair to look at Jamie. "Do I need to go get Scott and make him cheer you up?"

Jamie shook her head.

"What, is he the reason you're crying?"

Jamie sniffed and looked to Amy, holding up the letter. "He loves me and he spoke more in a paper than anyone ever has." Tears running down her face she reached for her phone.

> I love you, Scott. I always will.

Five Years Later

Jamie smiled and looked at Drew. He had stopped being Doctor Bond to her long ago, and she only used the moniker when she wanted to tease him; much like he did to her.

"Sorry," he said with a chuckle. "It's my last chance. Mrs. Scotch doesn't roll off the tongue as well."

"I don't know. I kind of like it."

"So, are you ready?" he asked, holding out his arm for her to take.

Jamie smiled and wrapped her arm in his. "I'm more than ready."

It had been five years since she had meet Drew, Scott, and Duncan. Five years, and so much had happened. Sometimes it felt like a lifetime, sometimes she would swear she had just arrived on campus. Five years, and a lifetime at once.

Two ushers stood on either side of the sanctuary doors, and with a nod from Doctor Bond, they opened the door and the bridal march began to play. Amber stood as her maid of honor and gave Jamie a thumbs up before she turned and began the walk. She was the same age now Jamie had been when they met and getting ready to head to college herself. Once she reached the front of the chapel and took her place, Jamie took a deep breath and took her first step.

Everyone in the small church stood to their feet and turned to watch her enter.

She walked in a euphoric haze. Five years. Just five years, and she wondered how she could have asked for a better life.

"Perfect is what you make it. You can be happy without being perfect."

Scott had told her that once, and at the time she hadn't understood. He had taught her to love her life, enjoy the moment, and don't hold on to the things that make you unhappy. She had hung on to that choice and eventually found a balance with her aunt and uncle. Their relationship wasn't amazing, but it was better. And they were there, to watch her marry her best friend.

In the pew in front of them, along the aisle, stood Beth Bond. Seven months pregnant. Doctor Bond would have a second chance at a child of his own. He was stronger and healthier, and Jamie kept a stern eye on him to ensure she'd never risk losing him again.

Jamie looked to the front of the church, and her breath caught.

Scott stood, waiting for her, a wide smile on his face. He was so handsome in his black tuxedo, so tall and strong. Her strength. Behind him stood Duncan as his best man, and beside Duncan Scott's friend Drake Casey. Duncan had grown up in five years and found out there was more in the world than just him. He was in medical school, and Jamie bet he wasn't more than a year away from getting married himself, to a great girl named Corinne.

But, Jamie only focused on Scott. In minutes, he would be her husband.

"You're beautiful," he whispered when they reached him.

She couldn't say anything. Her heart was too full.

Pastor Eason, who had been Scott's pastor nearly his whole life, smiled at them both before he looked out over the congregation. "We are gathered here today in the face of God and this gathering of family and friends, to join together Scott Taylor Scotch and Jamie Danielle Boyer in matrimony; which is an honorable and solemn estate and therefore is not to be entered into unadvisedly or lightly, but reverently and soberly. Scott and Jamie have come now to be joined. If anyone can show just cause why they may not be lawfully joined together, let them speak now or forever hold their peace. Who gives this woman to be married to this man?"

"I do," Drew said and turned her to face him, his eyes glistening. He lifted her veil from her face and kissed her cheek. "You have made me so proud."

"Thank you for being everything to me," she whispered, then smiled. "Doctor Bond, may I give you a hug?"

He laughed and wrapped her in a warm embrace. Jamie turned back to the altar and to Scott. She took his outstretched hand, and they took the first few steps together. Facing the world side-by-side.

As cheesy as it sounded, she finally knew the best dreams had come true.

The End

About Katie Charles

Katie Charles lives in Kansas City with her family: husband Daniel, stepdaughter Katie, and biological daughter Maebh.

She has three dogs: Eloise a Chihuahua pug mix, Sasha a Boxer Mastiff mix, and Kenna a Cavalier King Charles Spaniel. They also have a cat, Kitters an orange tabby.

When not writing Katie can be found reading, crocheting, watching Blippi and Meekah, or teaching high school science at her day job.

See more at KatieCharles.com